I0626141

*Advance praise fo,*
The Evolution of Reptilian Handbags
and Other Stories

"Melanie Lamaga's stories are magical, but they're not the same old magic. Old magic is made new again, and new magic blooms in the most unexpected places. With a remarkable range for a slender volume, these stories are delightful, moving, and just plain fun."

—Dennis Danvers, author of *The Circuit of Heaven*

"Melanie Lamaga's stories are richly imagined, delightfully various, subtle, mysterious, humane, and very welcome additions to the growing canon of the American Fantastic."

—Tom De Haven, author of *It's Superman!*

"Melanie Lamaga's stories are weird, wry, startling and passionate. The reader stands entranced on a rocky headland, watching sleek marvels crest the surface all around."

—Andy Duncan, author of *The Pottawatomie Giant
and Other Stories*

"A collection of beautiful, eerie stories that hover on the cusp between nightmare and sunlit dreaming, the everyday and the never-was, Melanie Lamaga's striking debut will appeal to readers of Karin Tidbeck, Kelly Link, and other writers who explore the literary twilight country of our unspoken fears and desires."

—Elizabeth Hand, author of *Available Dark
and Errantry*

# THE
# EVOLUTION
## OF
# REPTILIAN
# HANDBAGS

AND OTHER STORIES

# THE
# EVOLUTION
# OF
# REPTILIAN
# HANDBAGS

## AND OTHER STORIES

## MELANIE LAMAGA

Metaphysical Circus Press
*Richmond, VA*

Requests for permission to make copies of any part of the work should
be submitted online to editors@metaphysicalcircus.com or mailed to the
address below:

Metaphysical Circus Press
912 West 49th Street
Richmond, VA 23225
www.metaphysicalcircus.com

"Waking the Dreamer," previously published by The Metaphysical Circus, 2012
"Medusa," previously published in *Zahir*, 2010
"Invisible Heist," previously published in *Fiction International 38:
Sacred/Shamanic*, 2005
"Mr. Happy the Sharpshooter" previously published as "Mr. Rogers the
Sharpshooter" in *An Alternate Universe*, 2001

Quotations from Kabir taken from *One Hundred Poems of Kabir*, translated
by Rabindranath Tagore assisted by Evelyn Underhill, 1915

ISBN: 978-0-9899772-0-3
Library of Congress Control Number: 2013920934

Cover art and illustrations copyright © 2014 by Sophia Hermes (with
the exception of the alligator illustration in "The Evolution of Reptilian
Handbags," which is in the public domain).

Typesetting by Jill Ronsley

Text set in Goudy Old Style

Printed in the United States of America
First Metaphysical Circus Press edition, 2014

*For my family, with love*

# CONTENTS

# What Kind Are You?

"There are more things in heaven and earth, Horatio,
than are dreamt of in your philosophy."
—William Shakespeare, *Hamlet, Prince of Denmark*


WHEN I REMEMBER DUNDALK, MARYLAND, I think of the Fish
Pub: splintered wood floor, blacked-out windows, swinging
red doors, the only light from beer signs glowing red, white
and blue.

I grew up in a row house with a concrete stoop. I wore a
white shirt and plaid skirt like every other girl in school. My
folks worked at Industrial Steel. Point is, our lives were normal, far as I knew.

My last night in Dundalk started out normal, too. Just me
and Ray and the rest of what we called the Fish Club, playing
pool. Except Frank was dead by then, so it couldn't have been
normal at all. Funny how your memory tries to smooth the
rough edges.

Rewind. Tell the truth.

My last night in Dundalk, everybody was drinking way too
much. Frank was dead, Ma had disappeared, and my fiancé

was flirting with the bartender. But all of this still seemed random, separate from my real life.

Then all hell broke loose.

I'D BEEN WORKING AT WINGER Shipyard two years. The girl welder. That's what the guys called me when the boss was around. The rest of the time it was *Blondie, bring me a sandwich*, and *Hon, can ya help me light my torch?* and other hilarious jokes.

After Ray and I started dating, they eased up. Ray Mikos had smooth, olive skin and a beautiful face like those old Greek statues without arms, except his nose was crooked from falling out of a tree when he was ten. He wasn't tall, but nobody messed with Ray—and not just because he was a foreman. He was the type who kept everybody cool and got the job done. I liked that about him, almost as much as I liked the way he watched me with those dark eyes of his whenever I walked in a room.

After we got together, I found out he could get the job done in the bedroom, too. The way he used his tongue. He took me to the edge and kept me there until I screamed and grabbed his head.

By the time I turned twenty-one, me and Ray been living together for a year. The wedding was planned for the week before Christmas. Our colors were black, white and red. The church was going to be full of poinsettias.

Then one night at work, I got a call from Pop. Said Ma had taken off.

At first I couldn't believe it. But Pop said he found a note on the kitchen table under a beef and potato casserole, saying it's what she had to do and asking us to forgive.

After Ray and I got off shift we went over to the house. Pop sat on the couch, still in work clothes and boots. His gray hair bristled on his head like a scrub brush. Normally my pop stands straight as a soldier, but that night he looked like he was melting into the couch. He held Ma's note in one hand and a bottle of Jim Beam in the other.

"What happened?" I asked. "You guys get in a hellacious fight?"

"No! I swear." Pop shook his head. "She's been acting strange, but she wouldn't say nothing."

"Strange how?" I asked.

Pop shrugged. "Stopped going to her disaster relief meetings. Got quiet except for talking about your birthday. Worrying what to get you. Give her a check, I say. Let her get what she wants. But no."

I touched the necklace she'd given me: a silver angel, tiny and perfect right down to the feathers on her wings. At home I had a collection of angels—glass, brass, ceramic, you name it—all presents from Ma. It was our thing.

"Where's her family?" Ray asked.

Pop shrugged. "They came from Mexico before she was born, but they all died or left a long time ago. Crazy, blonde spics."

"Ma don't like that word," I said.

"Well, she ain't here." He took a pull off the bottle, defiant and heartbroke.

"I can't believe this." I flopped down on the sofa and took the bottle from Pop. "My wedding is less than three months away!"

"Faye's a good person," Ray said. "She'll be back."

I took a slug of the whiskey and shook my head. I'd never heard of somebody's ma taking off like that, a grown woman running away from home. And Pop was right, the last time I saw her she was acting strange.

It was on my birthday. Usually Ma went crazy with foil balloons, streamers and homemade angel-shaped cakes. But for my twenty-first there was just spaghetti and a chocolate cake from the grocery store.

I didn't think much about it at the time. After all, I wasn't a kid anymore. But after dinner, when I went to the kitchen to help Ma clean up, I found her holding a plate under the faucet, staring like she was in a trance.

"Something wrong?" I asked.

"You're twenty-one. A grown woman." She looked at me with this God-awful sad face that made her seem old. Usually people thought we were sisters 'cause we had the same *café con leche* skin, honey-colored hair and dark blue eyes.

"Well, for Pete's sake, Ma." I clanked plates into the dishwasher. "It ain't a funeral."

She flinched. "Don't say that! Some people in our family have bad luck."

"What kinda bad luck?" A glass I was rinsing slipped out of my hand and cracked in the sink. "Oops! It's starting," I joked.

Ma didn't smile. "Sometimes, when our people come of age, they change. Sometimes it skips a generation." She pushed back the white lace curtain and stared out the window. "I wish I'd gotten it, to spare you."

I could see her hands shake as she dropped the curtain, then picked up a dishtowel and twisted it.

"You're just freaking out over stories your mama used to tell." I remembered curling up with my silver-haired *abuelita*, listening to tales of shape-shifters and ghosts, and sipping cocoa with a hint of chili.

Ma nodded. "Mama wanted me to name you something different. We fought about it right up until she died."

I frowned. "What's that got to do with the price of beans?"

She hugged me, harder than she needed to. "I named you Angel to protect you. So don't worry, okay?"

"Who's worried? I'm fierce." I kissed her cheek and went back to loading dishes.

I didn't believe in luck; I believed in what I could see. But Ma read the *Weekly World News* and got really twisted about some of those stories, like the alien babies they said the government was experimenting on, or the female yeti who got shot by hunters in Russia. The story said a second yeti kept the hunters trapped in their cabin, howling until they gave the body back.

"Hm. Blurry," Pop had said when Ma showed him the picture of the yeti carrying his dead wife through the snow. "In this digital age you'd think somebody could get decent photos of Bigfoot every once in a while."

I guess Pop and me both snickered because Ma snapped, "Shame on you! Especially you, Angel."

"Me? Why me?" I squealed, still trying not to laugh.

"Because you're my daughter, and you best remember there are things in this world that you don't understand. Not everybody's lucky enough to fit in."

THE FISH CLUB GOT STARTED right after Ma left. We was all pretty sloshed, and Marcus decided it meant something that Frank, whose last name was Fish, hung out at the Fish Pub.

"Hey, that's true." Frank nodded slowly. He'd drunk so many shots of Jack he swayed in circles, even sitting on a bar-stool. "We're the Fish Club of the Fish Pub!" he yelled, and pounded the butt of his cue on the floor.

Frank Fish and I had gone to the same high school, but we weren't friends back then. I was the girl welder in shop class; he was the all-American jock with a pretty-boy face. Now he worked at his dad's car repair shop and had a gut like a beanbag chair.

That night we decided everybody needed fish names. I ended up Angel Fish, of course, and Ray got Sting Ray. We named Marcus Flying Fish because he was always popping up with some new obsession like building a DIY submarine or learning to speak Cherokee. We called him Fly for short, because he was stylish, with a wild 'fro that drove the older black guys at work crazy. They was always yelling at him to get a haircut or at least cornrows, for God's sake. He'd just grin and yell out, "Jimi Hendrix!" or "Weezie Jefferson!" or "Kareem Abdul Jabbar!"

CeCe was harder to name. "How about Catfish," I said, "because she's got those slanty green eyes." CeCe was a beautician, always dying her hair experimental colors. She was her own best advertisement—had the face and the figure, but not stuck-up at all.

"Why don't we call her Perch?" Fly said. "You know, on accounta she's lazy."

CeCe shook her head, swishing her violet curls. "I'm not a fish. I'm the sea, see? I'm the air you breathe, and without me you die. So watch yourselves."

"Come on!" I said. "You have to pick a fish."

"Names are important, Angel," CeCe insisted. "You let people call you the wrong one, you end up living somebody else's life."

I let this idea swirl around my brain awhile. "Are you saying your whole life is based on whatever random name your parents pick when you're born? What if they pick wrong?"

"Egg-sackly." CeCe widened her eyes.

Ray waved his beer bottle in a circle to get the bartender to bring another round, then turned to me. "So, what kind of angel are you?"

"Fluffy wings. Beautiful," I said. "What else?"

Ray shook his head. "That's just Hollywood bullshit. Truth is, you've got seraphim, cherubim, thrones, dominions, virtues, archangels, powers, principalities, archangels, and guardian angels." He ticked them off on his fingers. "That's not counting the fallen angels who left with Lucifer."

CeCe snorted. "How the hell do you know all that?"

"Church. You should try it sometime, heathen." Ray took a swig of beer.

"So what do all those different angels do?" I asked.

Ray gave me a long, dark look, and I knew why—I didn't go to church. It was the only thing we ever had a big fight about, but to me religion made about as much sense as Ma's *Weekly World News*.

"Angels execute God's will," Ray said finally. "You got your messengers, glorifying angels and avenging angels. They're like gladiators."

"Gladiators!" Fly yelled, jousting at Ray with his pool stick. Ray blocked him and spun away. Frank tried to join the duel but fell against the table. Glasses clattered and broke.

Our favorite bartender Bob, an Irishman with a goatee, yelled at the guys for being rowdy and told them to settle down or get out. Then Frank tried to pick up the broken glass and almost fell over.

"Fuckin' stop, man! You're gonna cut yourself." Bob came over with a dustpan and broom.

"No, no, no." Frank grabbed the broom and tried to figure out how to work it.

"Zombie logic," Ray muttered. That was our saying for people not knowing what they're doing or why, but hell-bent on doing it anyway.

While CeCe used her charms to get Frank to sit and drink some coffee, Ray swept up the glass and I mopped the floor. After that we forgot all about angels and what kind I might be.

Two weeks later, Frank Fish was dead.

FRANK HADN'T SHOWN UP AT the pub for a few days. We figured he was busy at the shop or his wife was pissed off at him again. Then one night the phone rang. A minute later Bob came over with that look on his face—the one you never want to see—and told us Frank drove his truck off a bridge somewhere near D.C.

Fly bolted to his feet. "He okay?"

Bob shook his head. "Sorry, man."

Fly kind of tilted sideways and Ray grabbed his arm to steady him. We all went to sit at the bar, trying to wrap our minds around it. Bob poured a round of Jack, on the house.

Fly downed his shot. "Me and the Fish Man been hanging since high school."

"Did Frank's wife say when is the funeral?" CeCe asked.

Bob winced and rubbed his forehead. "It was yesterday."

We all stared at him, shocked again. Frank Fish dead and buried. Not even a chance to say goodbye.

Later, when I called his wife to offer condolences, I found out why she didn't want nothing to do with us. Frank was drunk when he crashed. Instead of driving the ten blocks home like usual, that night he'd got in his head to get on Route 29 and head south.

"Nobody knows why," his wife said. "Do you?"

I said no and that was the truth. What I could have told her, but didn't, was that I was the last person he talked to.

THE NIGHT FRANK DIED WAS a Saturday. Nobody was in a hurry to get home after the Fish Pub closed, so we all walked down to the Z Diner for some breakfast. I remember feeling half-buzzed, half-sleepy, like you get after a night of slow, steady drinking.

After we ordered, Fly said he thought he might go somewhere next week. Miami or Charleston. He worked the loading dock at Winger and had a habit of using his sick days to take off to random places.

"Dude, you're gonna get fired," Ray said.

"But man, I gotta live!" Fly twisted his head to watch the waitress walk away in her short, blue-striped skirt.

"I think it's great." I poured a waterfall of sugar into my coffee. "I can't believe I never been anywhere. In seventh grade I was voted Most Likely to Discover New Worlds."

Ray tapped his spoon on the blue Formica table. "What does that even mean?"

I shrugged. "They probably made it up for me because I wanted to go scuba diving in the Bermuda Triangle."

Frank frowned. "You're a freak."

"No, hon," I said. "There's two hundred square miles of coral reefs in every color, full of shipwrecks and tropical fish. I saw a documentary in school."

"That's crazy," Fly said, impressed. "I'm going."

"Not me." Frank shook his head. "I don't want to be no alien experiment."

"Really?" CeCe blew delicately on her coffee. "Because out of everybody, I'd vote you Most Likely to Be Abducted."

"That ain't funny," Frank said.

"Ooo Hoo!" Fly hooted. "She's right. You look just like those dumb hicks you see on the TV with their eyes all big, talking about how the aliens stuck a probe up their ass."

"I vote you Most Likely to Get My Foot up Your Ass," Frank said, and dug into his eggs and bacon.

After we paid the check, CeCe and Fly left. Frank's truck happened to be parked on that block, so I asked him to give us a ride back to our car. "I'm too tired to walk," I said, yawning.

"Only if you don't mind sitting on my tools." Frank grinned. "Oops, that came out wrong. The truck's full of greasy parts and tools. Not sure you want to ride in there."

"I'll go get the car," Ray said. "Wait here with Angel?"

"Sure." Frank shrugged.

I flopped down on the bench outside the diner, looking up at the hazy stars. Frank sat next to me, but the weird thing is, no matter which way I twist my mind I've never been able to remember what we talked about. I only have this picture in my mind: I bummed a cigarette from Frank and he lit it for me with a match. Then he sat there and stared at the flame burning down. Just before it reached his fingers, I blew it out.

When Ray pulled up he said to Frank, "You okay to drive, Fish Man?

"Never felt better." Frank winked at me.

I got into Ray's car and Frank walked to his truck. As Ray pulled out of the parking lot into the street, Frank stuck his fist out his truck window and yelled, "Wallow!"

After Frank died, Ray told everybody he yelled, "Holler!" But he was wrong. I knew what Frank said, and he said it to me. It gave me a kind of secret rush, even though I didn't know what it meant—not then.

MY LAST NIGHT IN DUNDALK was the next Saturday, a week after Frank died. Bob had switched to day shift so we had a new bartender, Ava. Giant boobs and dark, shiny hair like a shampoo model. She told good jokes but I didn't trust her. Too sassy for my taste.

Ava proved me right that night—flirting with my man like I wasn't even there. And Ray was slurping it up.

Ray didn't usually act that way, but the guys had switched to drinking Jack in honor of Frank. The extra shots Ava poured on the house weren't doing Ray no favors, either. He got an attitude like I was acting jealous for no good reason and flirted even more to make a point. So I left.

Fly called, "Come on, Angel, go with the flow!"

I ignored him and shoved my way through the red swinging doors. CeCe normally would've left with me, but she was in the bathroom. I was too pissed to think how I probably shouldn't be walking alone at night.

It was pouring outside, harder than I've ever seen—a wall of water. I knew it would soak me in a second, but no way was I going back in the pub with some lame excuse about the weather.

I ran down the street past warehouses, trying to breathe without sucking in rain. I ducked into a narrow side street we used as a short cut to Hops In. I figured I could call a cab from there. That's when I saw a skinny, naked kid, twelve or thirteen years old, lying on the sidewalk, jerking around like he was having a seizure.

As I ran toward the boy, he flipped and slid into the street, a muddy, rushing river at least three feet deep. There was an open manhole, sucking in water, and the boy heading headfirst toward it. I grabbed his arm just in time to pull him back.

The boy shrieked, then gasped like he couldn't breathe. I knew mouth to mouth, but he was so thin and slick it was all I could do to keep hold of him. Next thing I knew, I slipped and we was both in the gutter, water rushing so hard I couldn't get to my feet without letting go of the boy. It took all my strength just to keep our heads above the water.

I screamed for help. Above us, I saw a blue-green light in an open window. A long, dark shadow rippled and slid away. It crossed my mind maybe the boy fell out that window, or maybe he was pushed.

I heard Ray yelling, "Hang on!" He raced down the street to us, boots sending up geysers of water, and pulled us both out of the water.

We ran back to the bar. While Ava dialed 911, Ray laid the boy, still thrashing, on the pool table.

The guys held him down and I performed mouth to mouth, my heart racing with adrenaline. I breathed and breathed, but after the boy stayed limp for more than ten minutes Ray pulled me away.

We stood there in shock. CeCe kept whispering, "This is wrong." I reached out to hug her, but she slid away. I sat down and closed my eyes, listening to her sobbing breaths.

I heard the outer door open. I looked over expecting to see EMTs, but instead a man and a woman ran in. They were tall and thin with pale skin, in gray silk clothes that reflected the colored lights behind the bar.

The man picked up the boy and rocked him back and forth. His eyes squinted shut and his mouth opened like he was crying, but no sound came out. The woman stood staring.

At first none of us moved. Then Ray went over to the woman. I didn't know what to say so I hung back.

"I'm so sorry, ma'am," Ray said. "Was he your son?"

"No," the woman said. "But in our care." She had a thick accent I didn't recognize. Eastern European, maybe.

"He was drowning in the flooded street. She tried to save him," Ray said, putting his arm around me. "But I think when we got him out of the water, it was already too late."

The woman's eyes got big. She let out a stream of words in

14

a language I never heard before, but I didn't need a dictionary to know she was cussing me out.

"I'm sorry. I'm so sorry," I whispered.

"Sorry?" she snapped. "Then what you were doing there?"

"I ... I did mouth to mouth," I stammered. "But I only had the one class, back in high school. I tried to—"

"You are liar!" the woman yelled. The man holding the boy began to wail. I was shaking so hard I'd have fallen down if Ray didn't have his arm around me.

"Ma'am, please," Ray said. He reached out to touch her shoulder, to offer comfort, but she jumped away like he'd tried to hit her and let out another flood of words in her language. Then, before anyone thought to ask their names or where they lived, the man and woman left, taking the boy's body with them.

I COULDN'T GET TO SLEEP that night, even though Ray rubbed my back for hours as we lay in bed. I guess I did sleep finally, because I had a dream. I stood on an empty street, rain coming down hard. Everything was gray—the pavement, the buildings, the sky—except way up high, a window shone with a bright aqua light.

As I walked closer, I saw a shadow on the rooftop above the window; then it jumped, wriggling through the air. The boy landed in the rushing gutter and I dived for him, but he slipped through my hands.

Instead of feeling bad, I felt relieved. I saw the boy swimming through a maze of tunnels, breathing underwater, escaping to the sea.

When I woke up, I jumped out of bed and ran for the shower. I wanted to feel different, feel clean. I told myself to forget about the dream.

Ray was still asleep when I went to get dressed. I thought it was weird because he always woke up when I got out of bed. As I stood there looking at him, I got a really bad feeling. He was lying on his back, not moving.

"Ray, wake up!" I yelled, but he still didn't move. For some reason I was scared to touch him, so I put my cheek above his mouth to feel his breath. Nothing. "Ray, God damn it, wake up! Ray!" I screamed right in his face. When he still didn't move, I knew he was dead.

At that point I kind of lost my mind, but my body kept going. Next thing I knew, I was driving past the docks toward the Fish Pub, squealing tires around corners, gripping the steering wheel. I had no idea where I was headed, but I needed to get there bad. Zombie logic.

I passed the Fish Pub and pulled into the side street where I'd found the boy. It was Sunday, no trucks or workers around. My mind was fixed on the window I'd seen lit up the night before.

I got out of my car and looked up. Black and blue clouds like bruises rolled off the harbor. I didn't see any lights in the building so I took a guess. Third floor, left.

On the third floor, a row of heavy steel doors lined the hall. They all looked the same, except the one at the front had a new brass lock. I knocked, and the tall, pale woman opened the door. She wore the same clothes as the night before, a gray silk dress that flowed to the floor.

The woman looked disgusted when she saw me. "What you want?"

As she glared at me, I realized I didn't know why I was there. The adrenaline rush that had propelled me out of the apartment was wearing off. My head swam.

"I'm sorry," I whispered. "I feel so bad about what happened last night, and this morning ..." I made myself say the words, "I think my fiancé is dead!"

"What you expect?" She crossed her arms and glared at me.

"What do you mean?" A wave of panic rose in my chest. "Why is this happening to me?"

"To you?" The woman narrowed her eyes and gave me a long look. "You don't know what you are, do you?"

I shook my head.

"Where your people at?" Her eyes shifted around the hall like she thought they could be hiding there.

"My pop's here in Dundalk," I mumbled. She waved that away so I went on. "My ma left about a month ago. Her family's in Mexico, I guess."

"Hmph," she grunted. "Well, go ask them." She stepped back and started to shut the door.

"I don't know where to look!" I reached out a hand to stop her, and she flinched away. I saw fear cross her face before the fierce mask came down again.

"I cannot help you," the woman said. "I know what you seem to be, but now you here, acting sorry." Her eyes narrowed. "Maybe you try to trick me."

"No, I swear!" I wasn't sure what she thought I was up to, but it didn't matter. I was desperate, drowning, begging for Ray's life in a language I didn't understand. "I didn't mean to hurt anybody." I clenched my arms to keep from trying to grab her again. "Please! There must be a way to fix this."

Something flickered in the woman's pale eyes, and for a second she looked at me like I was human. "If what you say is true ... if was a mistake, maybe you find way to undo for your friend. For boy is too late!" The woman's face twisted with grief as she slammed the door.

The clang of metal echoing in the concrete hallway hurt my head, but I was already racing down the stairs and out to my car. I had to get home.

Driving, I could only think of one thing—Ray, alive. That desire grew, inflating inside me like a balloon. I imagined shedding my skin like a worn-out Halloween costume, becoming something vast and hungry, knocking down buildings, erasing the sky.

My parking spot was gone, so I pulled into a loading zone at the end of the block and flew down the street toward home. It was October and the leaves on the scrawny trees had just started to turn.

A shrieking wind blew up out of nowhere, so strong it carried me about twenty feet then dropped me to my knees. By the time I got up the wind had passed, but every tree was stripped bare. All the car alarms were going off, and I saw half a dozen birds and rats lying in the trash and rust-colored leaves, all of them dying or dead.

Something moved inside my gut, tingling like the air before a thunderstorm. The wind, the animals—it gave me an idea.

I slammed through the front door of our building and spotted a giant cockroach on the wall. Testing my theory, I breathed in, feeling hunger, anger, need. As the roach fell dead I smiled. Then I heard a scream.

I don't know who or what I killed behind that wall. I wanted to scream, too, but I couldn't. Not yet.

RAY LAY ON THE BED just the way I'd left him. For a second I stopped, but I could still feel that crazy wind inside me. It pushed me on top of his body. It flew out of my mouth as I kissed him.

Ray's eyes snapped open and we stared at each other. "What's up, babe?" he finally said.

I couldn't think how to answer. Suddenly, I was dead tired. I rolled off Ray's chest and flopped back on the bed.

Ray sat up and scratched his head. "What day is it?"

"Sunday," I whispered.

"I don't feel right," he said. "I'm going to church."

I lay there while Ray showered. I couldn't move my body, but my mind raced with streams of thought I couldn't connect. I wondered what kind of life the boy would have had if he'd slipped through my fingers and escaped. The rush I'd felt when I gave him mouth to mouth—I thought it was adrenaline, but now I had the sick feeling that instead of putting breath into him, I'd taken it away.

I wondered if I'd somehow caused Frank's death, too. I'd blown out the match he held in his fingers. "Wallow," he'd said, like an inside joke. Then he drove off a bridge and drowned in less than three feet of water and mud. Some punchline.

Mostly I thought about Ma. Where she went and why she left. I wished I'd asked more questions when she said bad luck ran in our family. I didn't, because I thought the world worked like the line at Winger. Cut, weld, rivet. If you did it right, you ended up with exactly what you set out to make, the same every time.

But the world isn't like that. Lying there, I saw it as a seed or an ark. All possibilities were inside it: every creature that's ever been or ever will be, more than we could ever imagine, just like Ma said.

But what kind of creature was I?

I remembered the tingling energy I'd felt running down the street. It felt good. Like the first rush of your favorite drug. Like the best sex you ever had. Too good.

I heard the shower stop. In my mind I saw Ray's naked body, dripping wet. I could smell his clean skin, feel his heart beating—the life inside him that I'd put there. I remembered the taste of the wind as it flowed from my mouth to his. I wanted to taste it again.

I was halfway to the bathroom when I realized what I was doing. I loved Ray, but it wasn't love moving me toward him right then.

I forced my mind to see into the future. Past Ray's hands running up my thighs, his lips on my breasts. Past my fingernails etching into the smooth skin of his back. Past the salty-sweet smell of his neck, and the feel of him inside me. I saw us at the moment of climax, faces close, breath shared, a bright wind flowing from him to me. I saw his pleasure turn to fear, his face go empty gray.

Still, it took all my strength to turn around and go back to the bedroom.

I thought about what CeCe had said to me the night we started the Fish Club. "Wrong name, wrong life." Maybe it was just drunk talk, or maybe she meant what she said. CeCe usually did.

Before Ray left for church, he bent down to kiss me but I rolled over, shaking with the effort not to touch him. "I think I'm getting sick. You better stay away."

He gave me a long look and held out his hand. "Come to church with me, Angel?"

It almost made me cry. I wanted so bad for it to be that simple. But there were no demons to cast out. There was only me.

"WHAT IF YOU'RE LIVING THE wrong life?" I blurted. I'd waited until I heard Ray's car pull away; then I dragged myself to the kitchen and dialed CeCe's number.

"You mean, like your job or something?"

"I mean everything. Completely wrong life." As I said it, I thought I knew the answer. Maybe CeCe did, too, because she got real quiet. The sun broke through the clouds and poured in the window, making the walls look gold.

"That boy last night," CeCe finally said. "I think he was—"

"I know," I interrupted.

"I didn't know they really existed," she whispered.

"Me either. But I killed him, CeCe." I was gripping the phone so hard my fingers had gone numb and cold.

"Maybe," she said. "But it's not your fault. You didn't know what he was."

"It's not just him. There were ...."

CeCe took a sharp breath. "There were what?"

I got up and paced from the tiny kitchen to the tiny living room. Trapped. I couldn't bring myself to tell her what had happened with Ray and the animals, or my fears about Frank. "Just trust me," I said. "This isn't who I'm supposed to be."

"I don't get it." I could hear CeCe moving around her kitchen, clanking dishes, running water. The sounds comforted me a little, like this could be any day, any conversation. "You got everything you wanted. The union job, the guy, the ring."

"I know." I stood in front of my collection of angels with their pastel dresses and shimmering wings. "I wanted it to be real. But when you're not living the right life, even the good things don't make you happy. And the bad things are freaking insane. If I stay, it'll only get worse."

22

Part of me hoped that CeCe would tell me I was tripping, that I should have a Bloody Mary and everything would be okay. But she didn't. I heard her kitchen faucet shut off. Then silence.

"Ce, I'm right, aren't I?"

"God damn it," she snapped. "Why am I supposed to have all the answers?"

I paced back to the kitchen. "I'm just asking you what you think."

CeCe sighed, slow and deep. "The wrong things, they can weave together like a net. The more you struggle the more tangled you get." She sighed again. "Sometimes, you just got to cut yourself loose."

There it was. The truth. I closed my eyes and let it sink in. "I'm gonna miss you."

"Whatever, bitch." She was crying a little, but what she said was so her, so CeCe, that it made me laugh. Then she laughed, too, and that was better.

After we hung up, I started a pot of coffee. I still had a couple of hours until Ray got home from church. I shoved some clothes in a backpack along with my purse, toothbrush and shampoo. Then I started a load of laundry and cleaned the apartment.

When I was done, I sat down at the table with my coffee, trying to think what to say. I crumpled up half a dozen letters that told the truth, but when I read what I'd written, it sounded crazy or like a lame excuse.

Problem was, Ray wasn't like CeCe. He wouldn't figure it out on his own, and if I told him he wouldn't believe me.

Finally, I just wrote, *Dear Ray, Sorry to leave without explaining but sometimes it's better that way. It's not your fault. Love, Angel.*

It was the last time I ever used that name.

I KNOW WHAT MOST PEOPLE would say: Frank was just a drunk whose number was up, and a mini tornado killed the animals on the street. I can't prove Ray was dead that morning and not just asleep.

I can't prove anything, but I know what I know. I remember how the fish boy felt in my arms, how he fought me in the gutter, trying to get free. I can see what he saw as he was dying—coral reefs like sunken cities, rising from deep in a blue-green sea.

That's where I needed to go, too—away from the world of men. Cut the twisted lines of that life, and dive deep enough to find my true name.

# The Evolution of Reptilian Handbags

ONE FRIDAY, JOY FELL INTO A HORRIBLE TRANCE ...

HER FALL WAS NOT A metaphor, for metaphors had vanished long ago. Some people said they'd gone extinct, like bees. Others maintained they'd never existed in the first place, like angels or altruists. In any case, these days, falling into a trance was exactly the same as falling into a very narrow, very deep ditch.

Joy had been on her way to enroll in business school. Now she found herself sinking deeper and deeper into the trance, which was made of oil, water, and red and yellow food coloring like a lava lamp. Ugly mythological creatures—gorgons, chimeras and chupacabras—floated in the gobs of oil.

Seeing the annoying, psychedelic kind of trance she'd fallen into, Joy wished mightily that metaphors did exist so that this event could be seen as a colorful representation of her state of mind. Instead, it was her reality.

"Why?" Joy lamented. "Oh, why is it that every time I have a good idea of what to do with my life, something like this happens? How am I ever going to get ahead so I can buy a crocodile handbag large enough to contain a small, third-world country?" And with that she began to cry big, fat tears.

Joy's tears became part of the trance. They turned into swans and dived down to eat the green grass that swayed on the bottom of the ditch. The swans were so graceful, white and shimmery that Joy forgot to cry and started to wonder how she was breathing under all that goop.

### I WANT THAT ENORMOUS HANDBAG!

The shabby young man named Otto eyed the red crocodile handbag in the window of a fancy boutique. If he had a bag like that he wouldn't need an apartment. He could crawl inside it at night and fall asleep on the luxurious lining.

The two biggest problems in Otto's life were finding a home and finding women with whom to copulate. In fact, the two problems seemed to go hand in hand. Women liked nice places in which to copulate. That very morning his girlfriend had left him to go to business school so that, he suspected, she could copulate with other people in nicer places than he could currently provide.

Women like his ex-girlfriend also liked enormous reptilian handbags. Loved them, in fact. So Otto broke the boutique window and snatched the red purse, howling with glee because he thought he'd just solved his two biggest problems.

### UNFORTUNATELY, ACROSS TOWN ...

The mayor had just issued an edict against living in handbags. Simply too many people had begun using their handbags for shelter, and it was cutting into tax revenues.

Of course, the homeless people were not living in fancy designer handbags; their handbags were secondhand knock-offs made by children in third-world countries. But still, very large.

Satisfied with his day's work, the mayor decided to have a steak to reward himself before going home to copulate with his wife.

### BUT WHAT THE MAYOR DIDN'T KNOW WAS ...

At that moment, his wife Winifred was boarding a plane with her lover (formerly their maid), destined for a small, third-world country on a high mountain plain. There the couple planned to raise chickens and llamas, and paint mythic animals on the sides of handbags so tiny that only one bean could fit inside them.

At first Winnie had been skeptical of this plan. "Enormous handbags are all the rage!" she'd told her lover, Esmeralda. "No one will buy a purse big enough for only one bean."

"Ah," Esmeralda had replied, "but you are wrong, *mi amor*. The excesses of the past are fast catching up with your countrywomen. There is a wave cresting behind them, full of the *basura* of the past one hundred years: Tupperware without lids, mismatched shoes, millions of plastic water bottles and billions of tiny screws."

"Oh my!" said Winnie. "That does sound unpleasant."

"*Si*." Esmeralda nodded. "After that wave breaks, everyone will be up to their designer asses in so much trash that the very thought of enormous handbags will turn their stomachs, I promise you. And that is when we make our move."

## Soon, civilization collapsed!

Just as Esmeralda, the maid-turned-impresario had predicted, it ended in a tsunami of trash. The oceans belched their Texas-sized garbage patches back onto dry land. Plastic bags hung like jellyfish from every tree, and water bottles returned like salmon to the places of their birth.

The survivors wished so mightily that *drowning in your own trash* was a metaphor, the collective force of their desires brought metaphors back into the world. Of course, this did not remove the trash from anywhere but people's lungs. But folks took comfort in knowing that *kindling a relationship* no longer created third-degree burns, and when it *rained cats and dogs* no one would get bitten, and so forth.

Joy emerged from her horrible trance. The mountains of trash made the colorful goop and ugly mythological creatures look quite charming by comparison. Sadly, they were only metaphors now. Joy had no choice but to trade in her cute shoes for heavy boots, useful for kicking aside garbage.

Otto put wheels on the bottom of the enormous red crocodile handbag, hitched it to a dappled horse named Karma, and started a trash collection service. Not only did Otto enjoy his work, he found plenty of women with whom to copulate, for these days removing trash was just about the sexiest thing anybody could do.

Esmeralda became the wise mayor of the small third-world country whose elevation and lack of Tupperware and bottled water had left it one of the few pleasant places remaining on earth. This also worked out well for Winnie, who had enjoyed being a mayor's wife, except for the inconvenient fact of the mayor himself.

Winnie and Esmeralda spent their nights metaphorically devouring each other. Days, while Esmeralda participated in collective governing, Winnie fell into lovely trances and painted gorgons and griffins onto handbags made from the skins of small, desiccated blue lizards. The bags were large enough to carry only a single bean, or one of the tiny screws that, once upon a time, had held the world together.

# Mr. Happy the Sharpshooter

**MAY 1, 1931. CORYDON, PENNSYLVANIA.**

SLIDING EASILY, JOYFULLY, LIKE A seal down a waterfall, Frank Happy left the dark world and entered the bright.

A placid baby, Frank seldom cried. Watching shapes flow across the screen of his mind, he learned to interpret shadow and light. From symphonies of noise he plucked the tones of his parents' voices.

In the yard behind their white Dutch Colonial, Frank's father Ralph threw him into the air. "Look at my boy! Look at him fly!"

"Ralph, be careful!" his mother Bella called. But Frank wasn't scared. He laughed as he flew, breathing the music of trees and sky.

### 1935. FRANK, AGE FOUR, STEALS A DOLL.

She belonged to his cousin Cindy, who said he mustn't touch. So Frank sat in a corner and watched the girls play house.

He'd never seen a toy so real. The doll had a frilly dress, curly hair and eyes that closed when you put her to sleep. Like magic! When Cindy and her sister went outside, Frank spirited the doll away to his room and put her in his aquarium with the silver fish.

In the water, the doll became Dana Bo Ann, the Fish Queen. She told her subjects about another land. "In the Dry World, people don't have fins or tails. They have to walk, not swim." Then a hairy hand descended, snatching the Fish Queen away.

"Boys don't play with dolls," Frank's father snapped. "Understand?"

He flung the sopping doll across the room. She hit the mirror and fell, arms and legs askew, one eye staring off to the side. Not magic anymore. Frank gazed at his distorted reflection in the dripping mirror.

After Frank's father left, the thin, sandy-haired boy in the mirror reached for the doll, smoothed her dress and sang her to sleep. Frank watched until he heard his father's voice boom from the other room. Then he strapped on his soldier's helmet, snatched the doll and stomped on her until she broke.

When Cindy found the mangled doll in the backyard under a tree, she cried for an hour. Frank cried, too—down in the basement where no one could see.

**1939. FRANK, AGE EIGHT, PLAYS DRESS-UP WITH LARA.**

Lara had eyes like warm cocoa, hair like his mother's black silk dress, and a trunk full of dress-up clothes. Lara had moved to Corydon all the way from Philadelphia. She said the kids around here were boring, and she didn't care.

Frank didn't want to care, either. So when Lloyd Jones from across the street came over to get up a game of tag, Frank said, "No, thanks."

Lloyd, a stocky boy with freckles and red hair, had a mean streak—just as likely to shove you down as tap you when he was "it." Catching Lloyd's sideways glare, Frank lied, "I gotta go help in my dad's store."

After Lloyd left, Frank and Lara played *Alice's Adventures in Wonderland*. Frank became the rabbit in a coat with tails. Lara chose a lace dress that billowed like wings as they fell down the hole—the laundry chute—and landed on a pile of clothes.

The cat door became the passage to the garden. Frank made up a song. *If you're too big, you're stuck in the hall. If you're too small, you'll drown without the key.* As they marched through the kitchen, Lara's mother, frying chicken, cried, "Off with their heads!"

At suppertime, Frank launched himself off Lara's porch, head bursting with stories. Across the street, Lloyd crouched over his army men, throwing dirt in the air as he made explosion noises. Still humming his song, Frank smiled and waved.

"Liar!" bawled Lloyd, eyes scrunched like fists. "Sissy plays with girls!" Lloyd flung a handful of dirt toward Frank, stomped into his house and slammed the door.

Marooned in the gray dusk, Frank wondered how he got there. White houses, bare trees, brown grass. He felt as if his body belonged to someone else.

Frank looked back at the golden glow pouring from the windows of Lara's house. Sails unfurled as the house became a ship and glided into the night. He wanted to dive into the frigid waters separating him from the light, but he felt his father's eyes on his neck.

In the kitchen, Ralph stood rigid. "Dress-up is for babies, son. Are you a baby?"

"No, sir," Frank mumbled, "but Lara's mom said—"

"Don't sass me, boy!" His father grabbed his arm. "I don't give a damn if they drink horse piss and stand on their heads.

In this family we act right. From now on, you play outside with the other boys. Understand?"

A distant roar like surf pounded in Frank's ears. He stared at the back of Bella's neck where a few tendrils of auburn hair had escaped her bun and curled in the steam from the stove. His mother would understand.

Bella turned. "Frank, answer your father." The spoon in her hand dripped tomato sauce onto her yellow apron with blue flowers.

Frank took a breath, eyes wide. Before he could pour his feelings into words, his father snapped, "That's it!" and yanked down Frank's pants.

Frank shrieked as his father spanked him. Hysterical, outraged, he lost control of his bladder and peed on the floor. Even after Ralph deposited him into Bella's arms, Frank kept shrieking. Finally his father poured a cup of water on his head.

"Something wrong with that boy," Ralph said. He wiped his hands on a dish towel and threw it into the sink.

Frank's mother put him in bed and stroked his forehead until he drifted off into a vast, dark lake. The water teemed with electric eels that stung his legs, pulling him down.

As he slipped under, Frank saw Lara waving sadly from the stern of a boat—skin moonlight silvered, hair swirling like night birds.

---

The next day Frank remembered he'd been spanked, but the details had washed away, leaving only a smear of shame. At breakfast his father didn't look at him.

From then on, Frank played outside with the other boys just often enough to keep his father satisfied. Mostly, he stayed inside playing guitar and writing stories.

*Zol was a quiet boy with a twin sister named Zoey. They shared a special talent—the ability to talk to animals. One day an evil man with a hammer-shaped scar killed their parents and kidnapped Zoey. A crow named Midnight saw the whole thing.*

*Wandering through the forest, Zol and Midnight ask the animals they meet if they have seen Zoey. Along the way they find children in trouble and save them from bullies and thieves.*

Frank crafted puppets from papier maché and used them to act out his stories and songs. Performing in the mirror, he remembered how he used to believe a different Frank lived on the other side. He knew it couldn't be true, but still he liked to pretend.

The boy in the mirror always looked happy. Puppets danced wildly on his hands as he sang. His voice rang in Frank's head like a bell.

When Lara invited Frank over to play, he made excuses. Eventually she gave up. Then she joined the laughter when Lloyd and the other boys called him Fancy Frank, dancing on tiptoes to mimic his buoyant walk.

Frank just looked at the sky and hummed under his breath. He'd become accustomed to floating alone, skin growing reflective scales, arms and legs sprouting fins.

**May 1, 1941. Frank's father gives him a rifle.**

Frank tore the silver paper from the long thin box and tried to guess what could be inside. A spyglass? A magician's staff? When he saw the rifle, his shoulders slumped; then he noticed the excitement spilling from his father's face.

"This is a Winchester 1894. Belonged to my daddy. Now it's yours."

In the weeks that followed, Frank discovered the gun was a magic wand, after all, opening doors into his father's world. Ralph taught him how to hold it and clean it. Saturdays they went out to Mr. Stanley's fallow field and practiced shooting.

*In a dusty market, Zol meets a one-armed girl crying by the well. The other kids torment her, even though she can weave beautiful rugs using her one hand, her feet and her teeth. She's so lonely she wants to kill herself until Midnight teaches her to weave magic earmuffs that turn insults into music and—*

"Frank!" his father barked. "You got oatmeal in your arms."

As Ralph adjusted Frank's stance, Frank glared at the glass bottle targets. He imagined Lloyd Jones mock-sashaying by and calling out in a falsetto voice, "Fancy Frank!"

*Pow-pow!* Lloyd's head flies off his body into the air, turns in circles, sprouts wings. It lands in a tree and becomes an owl perching on a branch. *Gotcha, Lloyd!*

As Frank pulled the trigger he felt a connection between his testicles and the target, so strong that it gave him an erection. The bottle shattered and Ralph hollered. Inside, Frank went still. "That was easy," he heard himself say.

"Easy?" Ralph snorted. "Let's see you do it again!"

Frank took aim at another bottle and hit. His father moved him farther from the targets, but space had collapsed. One by one, Frank felt the bottles explode in his head, bits of glass flying skyward, catching the sun.

As the last bottle evaporated, Frank lowered his arms and dropped the gun. Ralph grabbed him in a bear hug, roaring over and over again, "That's my boy!"

———

The day after Thanksgiving, Frank left with Ralph and the other men for his first hunting trip in the Pennsylvania Highlands. By late afternoon, snow was falling. Frank floated behind his father as they snaked along the edge of a frozen lake.

*Gliding silently through the misty forest, Zol tracks the man with the hammer-shaped scar. He'll rescue Zoey and shoot the man with his magic shrinking gun until he's too small to hurt anyone ever again.*

Suddenly Ralph dived, jerking Frank down with him behind an outcropping of rocks. Peering over the top, Frank saw a huge buck knocking the ice with its hoof. Its shoulder muscles rippled as it bent its head to drink.

"He's all yours," Ralph breathed into Frank's ear.

Frank watched, mesmerized. The buck swung its antlers, blowing steam and droplets of water as it scanned for danger through the falling snow.

"Do it now, damn it, or I will!" Ralph's whisper had a ragged urgency. Frank lifted the rifle and shot wildly. The buck leaped into the air.

"Goddamn it, you got him!" Ralph bellowed.

"He ran away," Frank whispered.

"They don't always fall where they're hit, son. We gotta track him!"

Frank staggered to his feet and followed his father. *It can't be true. I aimed to miss. It can't be true. I never miss.* The mantra repeated in his head as he ran. When Frank saw the fallen buck, tongue protruding from its mouth, he fell too and vomited.

"Shake it off, boy!" his father said.

Frank tried to stand, but overcome by dizziness, plunged back into puke and snow. Finally, Ralph carried him back to camp. He told the men, "Boy's got some kind of flu. Even so, he managed to shoot a twelve-pointer."

Ralph stripped off Frank's fouled clothes, wrapped him in blankets and put him on a cot by the fire. In his dreams, Frank hunted through snowy woods. Instead of a buck, he spotted the other Frank staring across the frozen lake, pity in his face. "Go away!" he screamed, but the specter remained. *It's him or me,* Frank thought. He took aim and pulled the trigger, again and again.

### DECEMBER, 1941. AFTER PEARL HARBOR FRANK GUARDS LARA.

Terror had infected sleepy Corydon. Every night Frank fell asleep watching Lara's darkened house, rifle by his side.

Ralph was drafted but declared unfit for service due to a weak heart. Enraged and ashamed, he formed a posse with Frank and the other boys whose fathers had gone to war. He called them victory hunters.

"The soldiers need leather," Ralph told them. "Shoot as many bucks and elks as you can. Small game, too. We'll divvy the meat to all the families in town."

The first year, Frank threw up every time he killed something. Even though hunting had become a sacred duty, he couldn't reconcile the finality of the animals' deaths with the beauty of their motion, the shapes they made against the sky.

Lloyd laughed and called him the Hurling Champ, but Frank shrugged it off. Lloyd was zit faced and a lousy shot, besides. Frank saw Lara's nose twitch with disdain every time Lloyd passed by.

## JUNE, 1949. FRANK GOES TO WORK AT HIS FATHER'S STORE.

Freed from the social structure of high school, Frank and Lara formed a tentative friendship, discussing books and movies over the verbena hedge that separated their backyards. By July they were drinking rum and coke on Adirondack chairs beneath the oak in Lara's backyard.

Through the long, bright summer evenings they talked about abstract expressionism, jazz and Temple University, where Lara was going to study art in the fall.

"You should go too, Frank," Lara said. "You could study music."

His eyes widened. "What makes you think I'd do that?"

"I've heard you playing the guitar and singing when your parents go out."

"It's just a hobby." Frank frowned and gulped his drink too fast. Carbonation burned his nose.

"Fine, study something else," Lara said. "Anything!"

"Dad needs my help." Frank held himself very still. "He's planning an addition to the store."

"I don't understand you at all, Frank Happy." Lara sat up abruptly in her chair, startling him. Her hair swung like a curtain across the side of her face. "Don't you want to get out of this town?"

"Maybe next year." Frank stared up into the oak tree where sparrows fluttered among the darkening branches. He didn't tell Lara about the brochures in his desk, or the afternoons he and his mother had spent poring over them. Ralph said, "College is a luxury for people who don't need to earn a living." And that was that.

---

After Lara left for Temple, Frank immersed himself in writing new stories in the evenings.

*Zol and Midnight meet a frog that tells them Zoey is living under a lake with a clan of water witches. They ride dolphins like rockets, their long blue hair streaming out behind them.*

*Zoey says the witches saved her from the man with the hammer-shaped scar, and now she must live in the lake. Blue streaks grow in the dark hair that swirls and drifts around her face.*

*To reward his loyalty, Zoey gives her brother a magic blue stone. Zol uses it to build a town by the lake for orphans and children who don't fit in, conjuring multi-level tree houses, refrigerators that never empty, and beds that float like clouds. Fred the White Fox teaches the kids how to heal sickness with songs. The town is called Magic Land.*

Frank wanted to use his old puppets to act out the stories, but he feared someone would see. When his parents knocked, he shoved the notebook under the bed next to the rag he used to clean himself after masturbating.

Frank tried not to think of Lara when he performed that act, lying in his narrow bed at night. It seemed disrespectful, like taking something without permission. Instead he imagined a young woman like Lara (but not her) emerging naked from a clear lake. Waves of straight, dark hair rippled down her shoulders and back, dripping onto the curve of her rump. Her small, round breasts had nipples the color of chocolate, and crystal droplets of water clung to the silky triangle of hair between her legs.

Afterwards, Frank always promised himself it would never happen again. Oh, he knew other boys did it, too—he'd seen them passing around a magazine in the locker room senior year, making crude remarks and bragging about how many times a day they jacked off. But Frank didn't want to be like them. He would never be like them.

OCTOBER, 1950. FRANK ENLISTS IN THE MARINES.

The U.S. had entered the Korean War and Ralph insisted that Frank join up. The idea of shooting anyone horrified Frank, but his marksmanship trophies lined the living room mantle—a row of golden men poised to fire.

Night after night he lay awake, but he couldn't think of any way out. His country needed him. If he objected, people would think him unpatriotic, a shirker.

The day Frank reported for his physical, thoughts erupted and submerged like debris in a flood. He fingered his Buck knife, imagining his trigger finger cut off—a pool of blood on the floor, fear in the doctor's face. But as he stepped into the cold light of the examination room, the shameful thoughts evaporated like morning fog.

After enlisting, Frank realized with terror and elation that he had to tell Lara he loved her. She'd dropped out of college a month earlier, claiming to be homesick. Frank had hoped for more talks in the backyard. He'd planned to ask her out. But as the weeks passed he'd only glimpsed her staring out her window, eyes remote as rain clouds.

Frank knocked on Lara's door, shivering in the late fall air. In the parlor, they sat on the edge of the brocade couch as Frank told her he was leaving.

"I heard," Lara replied, distantly.

"Lara, there's something I wanted to tell you before I go. Something I've been thinking, feeling, for a long—"

"I'm getting married," she murmured, so rapidly that for a moment Frank wondered if he'd heard her correctly. "To Lloyd Jones."

Frank shook his head, bewildered. "But you despise Lloyd!"

Lara shrugged. "At Temple, Lloyd was there when ...," her voice drifted off.

"When what, Lara?" Frank reached for her hand but she recoiled, suddenly furious.

"Oh, you wouldn't understand! In the world things happen, Frank!" Lara ran from the room. A moment later, he heard a door slam.

Frank walked out into the hall and stared up the stairs, unsure of what to do. Lara's father appeared from the kitchen. His sigh echoed the scuffing of his slippers against the scarred wood floor. He gazed at Frank with opaque eyes and shook his head.

Frank left Lara's house feeling shaken and vaguely ashamed. Walking the streets of Corydon he tried to identify his crime, but it remained obscure—a dark, flickering shadow that swam below the surface of his mind.

JULY, 1951. PRIVATE FRANK HAPPY, SCOUT-SNIPER, SHIPS OUT.

On the voyage, Frank often fled the cramped quarters and the stench of unwashed bodies below deck. Topside he gulped salty air and reviewed his training—camouflage technique, map reading, and how to figure windage and elevation.

In Korea the summer simmered, fetid along the muddy rice paddies, dusty green in the hills where the battalion dug in. All the sniper rifles were assigned so Frank got a standard issue Springfield. There wasn't much action, anyway, and he spent most of the summer with a shovel in his hands.

Pain, vermin and constant thirst. The stink of dysentery and festering sores. Digging, sweating, Frank developed a rash that wouldn't heal. A constant, low hum of rage buzzed like a song he couldn't get out of his head.

In late August, the First Marine Division went on the offensive. By the third day, the artillery had shredded the vegetation, leaving nothing but the blackened bones of trees. Frank had been shooting non-stop. As he paused to reload, a Chinese soldier ran toward him, bayonet fixed.

Frank drew his K-bar knife, sidestepped, parried the soldier onto his side and plunged the knife into his neck. He smelled sweat and shit as he held the man face down, watching his legs and arms twitch.

Frank heard someone screaming. He didn't realize it was his own voice until First Sergeant Jacobs yelled in his face, "Gook's dead! You got him. He's dead!"

The sergeant thrust a Springfield with an M84 scope into Frank's hands and pointed. "Sniper on the ridge, three hunnert yards. Take him!"

Frank lifted the rifle, hands shaking. He closed his eyes and focused on the sound of his breath. Time slowed. The sound of exploding artillery, the clack of machine guns and the screams of dying men receded. When Frank looked through the scope, he spotted a hat with a red star over a perfectly formed ear, so close that it seemed he could touch it. *Like shooting bottles.* The ear exploded. A fringe of dark hair rose into the air like a wing.

After they took the hill, Captain White put him in for a medal and a promotion. In his report he wrote, "Soldier shoots like fuckin' Wyatt Earp."

The name they pinned on him along with the medal stuck—Wyatt.

46

Marching with his platoon to their new position on the line, Wyatt felt powerful and sharp. He was a wolf, able to see tiny movements along a distant ridge, smell kimchi clinging to the clothes of invisible North Koreans, hear air pushed by the wings of an F-86 at ten thousand feet. Every blade of grass, every rock, every blackened tree against the blue sky felt like an extension of his body. His feet pounded a rhythm in time with the chant in his mind.

*I'm alive. I'm alive. I'm alive.*

———————

When winter came the temperature plunged to freezing, then below. On patrol, Wyatt and his partner, a lean, red-haired corporal they called IQ, ran under cover of snowfall to outposts, fighting frostbite and hypothermia.

The observation points were equipped with landlines for reporting information about enemy movement, but there hadn't been any for weeks. The humming quiet felt unnatural and dangerous—a void magnifying paranoia and cold.

"Fuck are they?" Wyatt glared at the blank, white hills. "What're they waiting for?"

"Fuck knows," IQ muttered.

Wyatt caught a movement about six hundred yards out, silver against snow. He fired.

"Fuckin' A!" IQ swiveled the binoculars to find Wyatt's prey. "Wait ... what's that?"

"Think it's a fox," Wyatt mumbled. Shame warmed his neck.

"Shit. Thought we were getting some action. I'll take over."

Wyatt shoved his rifle under his coat to keep it from freezing and grabbed the binoculars. Scanning, he tried to tell himself it had been a mistake, but that was a lie. Every time his gaze floated past the spot he saw it—a bloom of blood against silver fur in a sea of white snow, white sky.

---

In spring the world turned green. Rain filled the muddy paddies where men and women in coolie hats bent over, planting rice. The humid air swarmed with mosquitoes. Wyatt and IQ were ordered to move forward from the outposts to infiltrate enemy territory. When they spotted activity they'd call in air support, then creep across the line again to watch the fireworks.

"Got 'em!" IQ whispered. He and Wyatt hung on the branches of a pine tree like snakes. In the village below, the strafing run drove soldiers out of burning huts.

"Yep." Wyatt squinted through his scope. "Told you the whole place was N.K." He squeezed the trigger.

The planes also delivered napalm, an incendiary gel that burned skin and muscle down to the bone. Wyatt watched men dive into rice paddies and come up covered with mud and water, still screaming. At that point he figured a bullet was mercy.

When IQ and Wyatt finished picking off stragglers, they dropped from the tree. Wyatt ducked behind a forsythia bush to piss, waving a hand to clear the mosquitoes that buzzed around his head. Through the scrim of yellow flowers he saw a huge mosquito target his partner's face. Oblivious, IQ stared into the distance.

"Damn, man, can't you feel that bloodsucker?" Wyatt laughed. "Big as a hummingbird."

As IQ flinched and slapped the mosquito on his cheek, his head exploded. Bits of brain and blood splattered the forsythia.

Wyatt dropped to the ground, wondering if he was dreaming. How could slapping a mosquito blow a man's head off? He waited, suspended. No sound except the rattling cicadas. No motion except the mosquitoes, swarming over the bloody mass where IQ's head should be.

Automatically, Wyatt's mind calculated the angle and distance from which the sniper had killed IQ. But the logic of this was overridden by the unshakable certainty that his partner would be alive if he hadn't laughed, hadn't pointed out the mosquito. Guilt waterlogged him, filling his body until he felt he would drown.

Wyatt lay motionless for hours. In the dark his senses slowly returned. He buried IQ's rifle and pack and wrapped his poncho around the remains of IQ's head, gagging back nausea and the urge to scream. Then he hoisted his friend onto his back and carried him back to the platoon.

## June, 1953. Frank leaves Korea, a hero.

Assigned to Force Recon, Frank spent the rest of his enlistment training at Camp Pendleton in California. Floating in inflatable boats, he learned how to gather intelligence and rescue hostages. As he tested his muscles night after night against the Pacific surf, the drone of rage receded. He wasn't Wyatt anymore, but he didn't feel like Frank, either.

In the moments before he fell asleep, he wondered where they'd gone—the boy and the sniper. He shook his head to dislodge the ridiculous notion. Of course he was still Frank. He'd just grown up.

---

At a Marine buddy's wedding reception in San Diego, Frank met Rita, a red-haired socialite from Los Angeles with a trim figure and blue eyes that seemed to glow in the dimly lit room.

Rita liked men in uniform. Frank liked the way she looked at him and the intoxicating smell of her expensive perfume. By the end of the night she had taught him the cha-cha. Three weeks later, they eloped and went to Mexico for a weekend honeymoon at the Rosarito Beach Hotel.

On Monday Frank had to return to Camp Pendleton to serve his last two weeks of enlistment. He closed the suitcase and glanced at the yellow adobe walls, the blue tiled floors and the rumpled bed. As he watched his wife applying lipstick in the mirror, his stomach churned.

"I can't believe I have to let you go already." Frank submerged his face in Rita's hair, breathing in her scent. His head spun with disbelief at his good fortune.

Rita turned her cheek for his kiss and sighed. "I know, darling, but this will give me time to arrange everything. I have my eye on a lovely little place on Sunset Boulevard."

"Is it very expensive? Because I was thinking—"

"Don't worry. Daddy will get us started. I'm sure he'll want you to work with him at Plastic Creation. He's always saying he needs a right-hand man." Rita turned back to the mirror and blotted her lipstick.

Frank thought for a moment; then he nodded. His dream of attending college on the G.I. Bill seemed childish now. Rita deserved a real man.

## 1954. FRANK ESCORTS HIS WIFE TO CHARITY EVENTS.

Rita loved to brag about Frank's Bronze Star and his thirty-three confirmed kills. *That was Wyatt,* he wanted to say. Wyatt seemed like a character in a movie, ruthless and precise—nothing like him. Still, Frank saw that it pleased his wife to show him off, so he swallowed his discomfort and chased it with scotch.

Days, Frank worked for his father-in-law Richard. He attended sales meetings and long lunches, nodding when Richard did, trying to bond with clients over sports and sexual innuendoes.

One evening, after a night of dancing at the Bel-Air Country Club, Frank sipped port while Rita, tipsy in a silk robe, carved roast beef for sandwiches.

"We're going to make beautiful children, Rita," he murmured. He imagined building tree houses and dollhouses, telling stories at bedtime.

"What?" Rita shot him a look.

"It's bound to happen, you know, the way we go on," he teased.

Rita frowned. "I don't intend to have children."

Frank rose and slid an arm around her. "You wouldn't like a darling little—"

"No!" Rita twisted away and hacked at the roast beef with venom. "You want to see me fat and bored, wiping bottoms and cleaning up milk?" The knife in her hand caught fragments of Frank's reflection, flashing like a code. "You might as well wish me dead!" As Rita whirled toward him, Frank reflexively grabbed for the wrist of her knife hand, but instead caught the blade, bone deep.

"Oh my God!" Rita dropped the knife and whirled into action. She wrapped Frank's hand in a dish towel—blood-soaked daisies on a sky blue field.

At the hospital, Rita told the nurse Frank had cut himself sharpening a knife. At home she fussed over him, solicitous and sweet. Frank tried to tell himself that he'd overreacted, but he remembered Korea, men with knives like cornered animals. He remembered Lara's eyes as she told him she was marrying Lloyd Jones.

He didn't mention children again.

### 1960. FRANK'S PARENTS CALL—CORYDON TO BE FLOODED!

The Army Corps of Engineers had begun construction on the Kinzua Dam. When it was completed, Frank's hometown would be inundated. Over the next two years, Frank wrote letters of protest and made phone calls to politicians—to no avail. In the end there was nothing to do but go home and help his parents move.

As Frank walked into his old bedroom, a numb, tingling sensation cascaded over him like the awakening of a limb that had fallen asleep. He felt a vague embarrassment, as if he'd stumbled into someone else's life.

Fortifying himself with sips of scotch from the flask in his pocket, Frank shoved books, games and crumbling puppets into boxes for donation. Then his hand fell on an old notebook. *Magic Land, by Frank Happy.* On the cover was a drawing of Zol and Midnight the Crow standing on the edge of a pine forest. Behind them Fred the White Fox ran toward a distant lake. Frank's ears rang as he sank onto the narrow bed.

"Come help me load the goddamn stove!" Ralph bellowed from the hall.

Frank dropped the notebook into a box and lurched to his feet. In the dresser mirror he caught sight of his father, eyes simmering with disgust, skin pearled with drops of sweat. Frank's stomach twisted as he realized the man in the mirror was him. He held up the flask and saluted. *Fucking flood it.*

That night Frank dreamed of Corydon beneath murky water. Winking shafts of light illuminated a roof here, a swing set there. Trash swayed in the weeds like muddy fruit. Frank saw himself as a boy swimming through empty streets.

———

Back in Los Angeles, Frank discovered that Rita's things—and most of their furniture—had vanished. As his footsteps echoed in the empty living room, his gaze fell on his collection of jazz recordings piled on the floor: Dizzy Gillespie, Count Basie, Billie Holiday. He breathed a sigh of relief before grief overtook him, roaring in his head like static at full volume.

Five scotches later Frank stormed the Bel-Air Country Club, ready for battle. Rita pulled him into an empty room, away from the stares of their friends.

"We aren't a good match, Frank. We just don't have the same values."

"Values?" Frank snorted. "All you do is flit from party to party. And don't tell me it's for the children. Let a real child show up and you run like hell, scared you'll ruin your dress."

"What do you care about, Frank?" Rita snapped. "Selling plastic? Staying half in the bag?"

Frank grabbed her hands. "I care about you, Rita. That's why I took the job with your father. I'm just trying to keep up with your set!"

Nostrils flaring, Rita jerked away. "You have no idea about my set. My father gave you a job and you've done nothing with it. If you hadn't been wearing that damned Marine uniform …."

Frank shook his head, confused. "Rita, please! I love you."

"You don't love me, Frank. You'd have to be alive for that." Disdain twisted Rita's face. "You may as well know I married you on the rebound. Remember your friend, Lieutenant Lark Stillwell? We met at his wedding."

Frank felt as if he was being dropped from high in the air into the middle of an ocean. The circular horizon encompassed nothing. No pain at first, just a dizzying freefall until her meaning hit. The spine-cracking impact made it hard to breathe.

"That's right." Rita nodded. "Lark is getting divorced. And so am I."

**1961. FRANK LANDS A SALES JOB AT A BOTTLE COMPANY.**

After his divorce, Frank moved to a furnished apartment in Echo Park. Evenings, he lifted weights for an hour, then drank at a nearby Irish pub, surfing the tide of bohemians, students and artists. Fascinated and repelled, he mostly kept to himself.

Months turned into years. Frank watched students become parents, soldiers become hippies and drunks get sober. He felt like a channel buoy, the only fixed object in a racing torrent.

Then one Saturday afternoon in 1969, he spotted Margo. Tousled dark hair, paisley mini-dress. Her amused expression suggested a joke or a delicious secret. Frank was on his third scotch—buzzed enough to start a conversation, not drunk enough to screw it up.

"Never seen you here before," Frank said.

"Just moved from Maryland." Margo grinned.

"East Coast," Frank mused. "The real world."

"The real world is overrated." Margo grinned again.

*Cheshire cat*, Frank thought. *Lara.* Normally this would have sent him into a dark swirl of regrets, but Margo's vivacious chatter distracted him. She told him she was a painter living at the beach with her daughter, and had a husband who traveled. "I believe in personal freedom," she trilled.

They started drinking together regularly. Margo entertained Frank with the theories behind her abstract expressionist paintings. Afraid to confess that he hadn't been to a museum in years, Frank nodded and snatched at fragments of long-ago conversations with Lara.

Sometimes they ended up back at his apartment. Half-drunk sex with Margo thrilled and terrified him, like being sucked down in the undertow of a crashing wave. Afterward he was never sure how he'd performed. When Margo disappeared for weeks, he churned in agonies of self-recrimination. Then, out of nowhere, she called and dared him to ditch work. "My house, four o'clock."

When Frank knocked, the salt-worn door creaked open. In the living room he found Margo's five-year-old daughter Joy, a dark-haired sprite in a purple velvet dress, perched in front of a television mounted in a walnut floor cabinet.

"I'm a friend of your mommy's," Frank said. "She home?"

"Store," murmured Joy, absorbed in an advertisement for a life-sized doll.

Frank spotted the bar and poured himself a scotch. Idly, he regarded the back of the child's tiny body, framed by the TV. When a program entitled *Mr. Happy's Magic House* came on, Frank wandered over and sat down on the couch. "I'm Mr. Happy, too."

"You are?" Joy clambered up beside him. "Have you been to the Land of Dreams?"

Memories of Korea sprouted in the back of Frank's mind. Flesh-dissolving bombs, head-exploding mosquitoes. He shook his head. "No. What's it like?"

"Watch!" Joy said, eyes bright.

On the television, a thin man dressed in slacks and a button-down shirt entered the living room of a rustic stone cottage. The cottage was furnished with purple velvet couches, and a cozy fire burned in the hearth. Peaked windows looked out over a forest of evergreen trees. As the camera moved closer to Mr. Happy, a wave of vertigo made Frank's head spin.

Mr. Happy put on a deep blue wizard's robe embroidered in silver stars and moons, and sang a duet with a crow puppet. *We're all friends, as you will see. Join us here in Amity. In Mr. Happy's Magic House, you can be who YOU want to be!*

Next Mr. Happy went into his laboratory, a sunny room lined with shelves of brightly colored beakers labeled with names like Joy, Laughter, and Creativity. In the slow cadence of a kindergarten teacher, Mr. Happy spoke about a sad boy named Ray who ran away. "Ray doesn't know that he's a unique human being, just like you, just like me. Let's go to the Land of Dreams and see if we can help him, shall we?"

Listening to the gentle flow of Mr. Happy's voice, Frank felt revolted, as if the man on television had reached out and licked his skin. He rose and stepped shakily toward the bar.

"S'matter, hon?" Margo breezed in wearing go-go boots, a paint-splattered tee shirt and orange hot pants. "You look like you saw an ugly ghost!"

Frank suppressed a shudder and waved toward the TV.

Margo ran a finger lightly down his wrist. "Mmm, Mr. Happy."

"Very funny." Frank poured another scotch for himself and one for her.

"He even looks like you. Sandy-blonde hair, high fore-head. But you're much more developed." Margo squeezed Frank's bicep and nodded suggestively toward the hall.

Frank took a deep breath and tried to shake the creepy feeling from his skin. "What about Joy?"

"She gets her Mr. Happy time, I get mine." As Margo led him to the bedroom, Frank heard the fox puppet singing. *I don't do things the way I should; I wonder if I'm just no good.*

JANUARY, 1970. FRANK WANTS TO FORGET MR. HAPPY.

When she'd had a few too many, Margo started to call Frank Mr. Sexy Happy. Their buddies at the pub picked it up, laughing and making cracks about Frank living in the Land of Dreams.

After a week of this he'd had enough. "I'm a Marine," Frank snapped. "That wimp is nothing like me!"

"Oh, I didn't know!" Margo looked sympathetic. "Were you in Vietnam?"

"Korea." Frank took a gulp of his scotch. Sweat trickled down his temple. "That man couldn't fight for a sandwich, never mind his country."

"Not everyone can be a war hero," Margo protested. "Mr. Happy's the artistic type. And he has a degree in child psychol-ogy. Joy adores him."

"Something's wrong with that guy," Frank snarled. "I can tell. Maybe he's a pervert."

Margo frowned. "What's the matter with you?"

Frank shook his head. He knew he should apologize, but he couldn't bring himself to make nice. *It's too much. Another goddamn shovel of shit. It's just too much.*

Though he downed scotch after scotch, Frank couldn't get drunk. That night, the ceiling above his bed morphed into a screen on which *Mr. Happy's Magic House* played endlessly. Fragments of the show took root and grew, choking other thoughts from his mind. The characters seemed familiar—a witch, a fox and a crow that sang, *Fly with me to the Land of Dreams, where nothing is ever quite as it seems.*

After a week of insomnia, brain buzzing with exhaustion, Frank called in sick and headed for the library. Crouching over the blue glow of the microfiche machine, he read everything he could find on the other Frank Happy.

*Born in Youngstown, Pennsylvania, May 1, 1931 to Ralph and Bella Happy. Age seven, began playing guitar ... only child ... made puppets for company.* One by one, the facts of Mr. Happy's life detonated in his brain. Their childhoods had been almost identical, except the other Frank had a grandmother who encouraged him to sing and play. The other Frank had gone to Temple University to study music. He'd been there at the same time as Lara.

Frank barely made it to the bathroom before vomiting yellow bile into the sink. He splashed water on his face and scrubbed it hard. In the mirror he looked haggard and green. *Mr. Happy.*

Frank burst out of the musty shadows of the library and staggered down the bright midday street. In every window the face of Mr. Happy accosted him, a distorted reflection in a stagnant pool. Mocking puppets emerged from adobe walls. As Frank ducked into the nearest bar, he heard the fox call out behind him. *There's never been a boy like you!*

**February, 1970. Frank sneaks onto the soundstage.**

Cradling the Springfield rifle he'd bought in a local pawnshop, Frank shimmied up the lighting scaffold at the Baltimore PBS station and hid. Watching Mr. Happy tape his show, Frank filled with a loathing so wet and thick he found it hard to breathe.

After the cast and crew left, Mr. Happy slipped out of his magician's robe and puttered around the set: humming, jotting in a notebook, touching up the paint on a puppet. When Frank was certain they were alone, he dropped from the scaffold onto the soundstage and raised the rifle in one silent, fluid motion.

He hadn't been sure how close he'd be able to get, so he'd bought a rifle with a scope. But this was better. He wanted to see Mr. Happy's face up close. Even more, he wanted the imposter to see him. Frank's heart beat fast as the man put down his paintbrush and turned toward him.

"Oh!" Mr. Happy's eyes flicked from Frank's face to the rifle. He took a deep breath. "Hello, friend."

"I'm not your fucking friend," Frank barked. "I'm Sergeant Frank Happy, First Marines. Real question is, who the fuck are you?"

"I'm Frank Happy, too," the other man said quietly. "But I never went to war."

"That's obvious. But I looked you up. The papers say you were born in the same state as me, on the same day, to parents with the same names. It's just not possible! You married a woman named Lara." Frank's voice broke.

"Oh," Mr. Happy said. "I see."

A wave of rage blurred Frank's vision. "Don't you dare pity me, you freak! While you were jerking off in college, I was serving my country in Korea. Thirty-three confirmed kills. I don't suppose that's something you'd appreciate, puppet man. *Vegetarian!*" Frank spat the word like a curse and gave a hoarse laugh. "You know, I want to throw up every time I eat meat. Always have. But I eat it anyway, because that's what people do. We shut up and eat what we're given. But not you, Fancy Frank."

Mr. Happy continued to gaze at Frank with such sympathy that Frank's finger automatically tightened on the trigger. *Not yet.* He wanted the other man to die pissing himself with terror, begging for his life.

"Let me make this clear," Frank said. "You are not Frank Happy. I am. You are a freak of nature, an abomination that doesn't even have the decency to be ashamed."

Mr. Happy shook his head, bewildered. "Ashamed of what?"

"Everything," Frank said. "Your wimpy voice, your girly walk, your silly magician's robe. Your existence slanders my name."

Sadness creased the other man's face. "I'm sorry you feel that way, Frank. But please, put down the gun. I know we can find another way."

"No can do, Fancy Frank. There can't be two of us. It's you or me. Understand? You're done." Frank cocked the rifle.

Blanching, Mr. Happy held up his hand. "I ... can I just have one minute?"

"Sure. Say goodbye," Frank sneered. "Guess you have a lot to lose. Family, career, fans." Frank had meant to twist the knife, but he heard the self-pity in his voice and cringed.

Mr. Happy gazed around the set like a parent looking at his child, turning slowly, taking it in. Midway he stopped, cocked his head and stared at the window.

Following Mr. Happy's gaze, Frank saw the backdrop rustle. The painted pine trees moved like real trees blown by the wind. Startled, he fired and the window shattered. Mr. Happy recoiled, shoulders hunching at his ears.

"How are you doing that?" Frank snapped. "Make it stop."

Mr. Happy took a deep breath and straightened his back. "I'm not doing it, Frank."

Frank walked to the edge of the set to investigate. He assumed the effect was created by some kind of projection system, but the soundstage behind the flat was dark and empty.

Frank glanced back at Mr. Happy. He'd half-expected the other man to make a run for it. In fact, he wished he would. A hunt—*that* he could understand. But the freak just stood there looking bemused, a light breeze ruffling his hair.

Frowning, Frank strode to the shattered window and looked out. A breeze, fragrant with the smell of pine trees, wafted through. From his high vantage point, Frank could see a lake in the distance shaped like the reservoir covering Corydon, but the water shone clear as glass.

At the bottom of the lake, surrounded by woods and fields of corn, his hometown shimmered, intact. Frank saw himself and Lara as children, swimming above the roof of her house, scattering silver fish. He saw the first buck he'd ever shot, picking its way through a petrified forest. The bubbles from its nose ascended—snowflakes falling in reverse.

Frank heard music, a simple tune in a minor key, and a torrent of memories washed through him. The wood polish smell of the parlor, the prickle of horsehair against his legs, fragments of songs and stories—Zol and Midnight in Magic Land.

Frank whirled around to see Mr. Happy playing the guitar. He'd thought the music was in his head. "I could have been the one to write songs and make up stories for children," he said hoarsely.

Mr. Happy stopped playing. "I know you could."

"How could you possibly know that?" Frank narrowed his eyes.

Mr. Happy smiled, sadly. "I saw you sometimes when I was a little boy. In the mirror. We told each other stories."

Frank's eyes widened. "My God! I remember you. Always so fucking happy."

"Not always, Frank," Mr. Happy said. "I was a lonely child, too."

"No! You got everything I wanted, and I got shit." Frank lifted the rifle to his shoulder. Space collapsed, and for a moment he had the sensation of being inside the other man, looking back at himself—eyes flat and cold as a mirror, rifle extended like a limb.

*It's him or me,* Frank told himself. But his finger on the trigger felt numb. The wind created a shifting halo of green in the window behind Mr. Happy; the bottomless sadness in the other man's eyes made his head spin.

Frank lowered the rifle. "What's the point? It's too fucking late. I had dreams, but they dried up and blew away a long time ago."

"Oh, no." Mr. Happy smiled. "It's never too late for our dreams."

"Don't talk to me like I'm a kiddy watching your show," Frank said wearily. "I've been around. I've seen things. It's dissolving me from the inside out." He weighed the rifle in his hands. "But you wouldn't know anything about that."

Mr. Happy nodded. "Maybe it's time I did."

"You? Yeah, right!"

The breeze rippled across Frank's face, cooling his fevered

skin. Drawing closer to the window, he laid the rifle down on the sideboard, opened the sash and leaned out.

In the sky a flock of crows flew ahead of monsoon clouds, tinted purple and gold. The vegetation below looked like Korea, bushes and grasses grown back since the war. Stooped men and women worked the rice paddies, and children flew kites painted with tiger medallions. Frank recognized a soldier he'd killed, eating a bowl of noodles under a tree.

Frank pulled his head back in and turned away. "It's not real."

"It will be if you make it real." Mr. Happy's pale eyes glinted in the setting sun. "I don't know why our lives were arranged this way, Frank, but I think maybe it's my turn to carry this."

"I just want to go home," Frank said, and then realized he no longer knew what that meant. The adrenaline had worn off and he felt tired. But the warm, piney breeze caressed his skin like a lover's hand. Insisting.

Frank stared at Mr. Happy for what felt like hours, but in the end may only have been the blink of an eye. The two men nodded at each other; then Mr. Happy held the rope ladder steady as Frank descended.

Mr. Happy picked up the rifle and watched Frank walk the path beneath the tree houses, their windows glittering in the liquid dusk. At the lake Frank stripped and climbed to a diving platform perched in a tree. A crow landed on a branch above him, flapped its wings once and settled.

Frank stared down through the silver skin of the lake, then launched himself into the air. He laughed as he flew, propelled by the echo of a familiar sound like the crack of a tree branch set free by a gust of wind.

# Waking the Dreamer

I HAVE A STORY YOU won't believe. No one does. And I planned it this way.

I know what I look like now, after so many years alone in the woods. But once I was part of the hustle and flow, a regular man like you. True, I had advantages—money and influence on my father's side—but I worked hard, too. They called me The Prince.

By the age of twenty-five I owned a railroad, a fleet of golden airships and a dozen newspapers. Originally, I bought the papers to facilitate my other businesses. At the time I had no idea how important they'd be to my real life's work.

THE SEEDS OF THIS WORK were planted just before my thirtieth birthday, unbeknownst to me. I only learned the details some six months later, reading the newspaper accounts.

It was the end of October, after a terrible lightning storm. A couple of young men, Maximilian Jones and John Maguire, were hunting deep in these woods when they discovered a naked woman lying in a secluded clearing. By her side stood a huge, white dog.

The young men called out to the woman, but she didn't move. As they approached, they saw a snake coiled near her head. Shouting, they rushed forward intending to kill the snake, but it slithered away into the leaves. They tried to drive off the dog, as well, but it barked and snapped so viciously they couldn't proceed. The young men didn't dare shoot the dog, for it had lain down across the woman's body.

Frantically, they rode their horses to the nearest town and made report. A police officer and a veterinarian associated with the SPCA were dispatched; but despite their efforts to entice the dog with chunks of meat, they could not get close to the woman.

A midwife who lived in the woods happened by and told them she could communicate with animals, sometimes.

"Oh, yes!" said Jones. "Please try."

The officer shook his head skeptically. The midwife closed her eyes for a moment and then announced that the dog believed it was born to protect the sleeping woman, just as his father and his father's father had done.

"Tell the dog we want to help her," the veterinarian said patiently. "If she stays out here like this she'll die."

The midwife shook her head. "The white dog says she must be left alone to dream in these woods forever."

"Ridiculous!" the policeman said. "All of you, clear out."

"Why should we be asked to leave?" Jones said. "We found her!"

A scuffle ensued, and Jones punched the officer. When restrained by the veterinarian, he began to curse and sob.

Although Maximilian Jones had no previous history of mental illness, this outburst marked the beginning of a breakdown. His family eventually committed him to an asylum where he resided for several years. His case is notable only in that he was the first.

The policeman's report indicates that having cleared the area, he lay down on the ground and shot the dog cleanly through the head. Of the snake nothing more was seen.

THE NEXT DAY A PHOTO appeared in the local newspaper, along with a short article. It said that police had rescued an unidentified woman in the woods outside Clarion, Pennsylvania. However, those who had first seen the woman told their stories to anyone who would listen.

Jones and Maguire claimed they had discovered a girl with raven hair and skin like a white rose. They felt sure she was under a spell that could be broken by a lover's kiss. Maguire vowed to kill the policeman for stealing the woman from him. The policeman claimed she was a beautiful witch, and blamed her for the failure of his manhood and his marriage.

The midwife opined that the sleeper was a vehicle from the stars, a biological library containing vast amounts of information that could transform the human race. The veterinarian theorized that she was an automaton such as those created by Vichy and Lambert in France, whose clockworks had started running low.

From these diverse seeds, myths took root and grew like tangled vines.

Soon the Philadelphia and New York papers picked up the story and published photos of the woman. The descriptions of her appearance varied wildly. Nordic men saw a pale-skinned blonde; Spaniards envisioned a dusky brunette; emancipated slaves saw an African woman with her hair in hundreds of braids; priests saw Mother Mary herself; and so on.

At the time I paid little attention to Sleeping Beauty, as she was dubbed by the press (first by the editor of one of my own newspapers, in fact). I usually had my assistant read to me while I ate or bathed, skipping all the fantastical stories about two-headed babies, monkey men and tentacled creatures from the deep—the usual tabloid fodder. It wasn't until I chanced to see pictures of the sleeping woman in a medical journal some months later that I became intrigued. Indeed, she was a beauty: a slender brunette with delicate features and pale skin.

I learned that the doctors at the hospital to which she'd been admitted had found no cause for her coma. However, there were physiological anomalies: eyes with slightly elongated pupils, an unidentifiable blood type, and a pulse so slow it seemed she must be nearly dead. Yet, as time passed she did not die or even decline. She remained as radiant as the day she'd arrived.

Word spread. Doctors and researchers came from all over the country and their bickering nearly led to blows as each attempted to claim her for his institution.

Among the general population the story had created a frenzy. Thousands attempted to prove she was their relative or wife. Those who prayed to her claimed miracle healings. A bishop sent to investigate caused an uproar when he declared that after her death she would progress swiftly to sainthood. In short, all who saw her, regardless of their education, social standing or creed, risked falling under her spell.

Observing the radical changes in visitors as well as his staff, the hospital administrator, Bob Roberts, realized the extent of the woman's influence. He considered transferring this inconvenient patient to another hospital, but the endowments providing for her care were mounting at an unprecedented rate.

Being a man of vision, Roberts resolved to adapt to this strange but lucrative new mission. He vowed never to lay eyes on the woman himself in order to maintain his objectivity and keep the hospital from collapsing into chaos.

WITHIN A YEAR, THE HOSPITAL had become a fortress. A massive iron fence, studded with black iron roses as big as a man's head and protruding twelve-inch thorns, surrounded the perimeter. Engineers installed hydraulic gates manned by a guard at the top of a tower overlooking the entire property. Inside, another half-dozen iron doors, each locked with a different combination, barricaded the sleeping woman from the world.

Perhaps the strangest feature of the new facility was the chamber in which the woman lay. The designer must have been one of the devotees of the Cult of the White Dog, which held that she should have been left sleeping in the woods, for he had created a forest of clockwork automatons: a dog that stood watch, singing birds with flapping metal wings, yellow bees that flew among crimson flowers, and a fox that hunted rabbits. Oak and willow lined the room, each green leaf waving as if in a gentle wind.

A pastoral scene, to be sure. But Bob Roberts assured me that if an unauthorized person were to break in, the bees, equipped with hypodermic stingers, would deliver a generous dose of tranquilizers while the rest of the mechanical army tore into the intruder with razor talons, claws and teeth. Even the leaves were as thin and sharp as a surgeon's scalpel.

Only a select few doctors and one nurse had direct access to the woman. The rules allowed visiting specialists to observe only, through multiple panes of thick glass. They came intending to take notes and confer, but often would simply stand and watch her hypnotically slow breathing, one respiration per hour.

THRONGS OF THE OBSESSED, DENIED access, gathered outside the hospital. They took up residence in a ragtag carnival of wagons and tents. Some attempted to bribe or blackmail the staff; others formed societies dedicated to dreaming, in the belief that while asleep they might meet her on her own territory. Stories multiplied; legends grew. Factions argued over such details as her origin, meaning and purpose.

I was one of the obsessed, I admit, but with a key difference. By that time I'd become one of the richest and most powerful men in the world, surpassing even my father. If I told you my name, you'd recognize it through the corporations and institutions I've founded. I still own them today, though no one knows this except my lawyer.

None of that matters. I only tell you so you'll understand—not only was I able to arrange to see the sleeper, we would be alone and unobserved.

On the day I entered her room, the curtains were drawn over the windows to the observation chambers. My own guards stood outside the door with strict instructions to kill anyone who attempted to forcibly enter and to stay outside themselves, regardless of how long I remained.

The mechanical forest was the one unknown. Even the designer could not predict or circumvent its actions, because in his enthusiasm to create and install the clockwork guards he had forgotten to devise a way to turn them off.

I wasn't concerned for I meant the woman no harm. Of course not—I was in love. To be on the safe side, I had donned a doctor's garb, complete with stethoscope and examination goggles.

The mechanical forest completely obscured the walls of the large room. The sunlight shining through the glass roof cast lacy shadows through the leaves. The huge mechanical dog approached me, twitching its silver ears. A steel and copper bird perched on the woman's glass box and cocked its head.

Impressive though the automatons were, I only had eyes for her. For a long while I just watched her breathe. Death didn't frighten me, but it took all my courage to move closer, reach out my hand and open the glass box.

A scent of indescribable beauty overwhelmed me and I collapsed. I caught notes of honeysuckle, baking bread, the skin of a woman I'd once loved, the ocean, pine trees—hundreds of scents evoking every good memory of my life, which I relived in complete sensory detail. I stayed like that for hours or days—I don't know—floating in the bliss that emanated from her skin.

Eventually, though my ecstasy remained undiminished, I became accustomed to my new state. Regaining the power of thought and mobility, I realized I still had not touched her.

I found myself on my feet. Shedding my clothes came as naturally as breathing.

If you're tempted to judge me, ask yourself this: if you could time-travel, be instantly rich, beautiful, famous, loved—that is, if you could actually possess the embodiment of your most sacred desire—wouldn't you? I knew this was no ordinary woman, but I am no ordinary man. She was my destiny. Of that I was sure.

As I lowered the sides of the glass box and reached inside, the hair on my arm stood up, crackling with static electricity. Gently, I untied the cords of the white linen robe that draped her body.

She was perfect. But this is a word, like "beauty" or "God," used to describe the indescribable, the unknowable. There are no words for some things because the immediacy and power of their presence transcend language, render it useless.

I had experienced something like this once before, when I was nine, the day I drowned in the ocean.

My father had taken me out in his sailboat. A sudden squall, a gust of wind, the crack of the boom against my back. I turned and turned, losing any sense of direction in my panic. I fought the pain in my chest, flailing against the blue-violet twilight.

Bruised water rushed over me, under me, inside my skin. Finally the pressure won, exploding into me as I breathed water in. I had an orgasm, the first of my life. The ocean became a rainbow of colors emanating from a light far below. Then a dark, elongated form swam up from the depths—up from the light. I thought it was a dolphin, but when it overtook me I recognized my father. He hooked me with an arm and yanked me out of the water.

I pondered the light at the bottom of the ocean for years before it occurred to me that it must have been the reflection of the sun above me, not below. Still, I had my doubts. I suspected that the watery man who took me from the ocean was not my real father but another father who'd replaced him that day.

I had dreams in which I fought him, prevented him from taking me out of the ocean, prevented him from pumping my chest with his wet, hairy hands until I vomited my bliss and let in the air that cut my lungs.

Father thought he'd saved me, but in truth it was too late. I had recognized this world and every sensation it produces as a fake, a poor imitation of another world, a perfect place that lies beyond our ken. That's why I found it easy to gain power, money, anything I desired—and yet it all meant nothing.

I'D HAD NO HOPE OF rediscovering the bliss I'd felt that day—until I saw her. Even photographs of the woman elicited a trace of the feeling I'd had in the ocean.

Now I stood naked beside her, mesmerized by her sleeping face. In her visage I saw everything I desired: beauty and humility, innocence and sensuality. Ecstasy coursed through me like a current, pulling me closer. I mounted her and penetrated the silken warmth between her legs.

All the strength immediately left my body, drawn out by her power no doubt, for I've always been robust in the act of love. I collapsed forward, pressing my lips against hers for one instant. Then her eyes flew open.

A jolt of electricity ripped though me, and I catapulted backward. My entire body throbbed with pain even before I slammed into the trunk of an iron oak tree and collapsed to the ground among pebbles of glass from the box that had shattered with her awakening.

Semi-conscious, I watched her beauty explode like a tree in a forest fire. Blue currents danced like snakes around her body, turning her skin reddish brown and setting her hair aflame.

Another security measure gone horribly wrong, I thought. Screaming, I leapt toward my beloved, planning to hurtle my body against hers and disengage her from the power source, or die in the attempt. But before I could reach her, the dog attacked me, teeth ripping into my skin. The rest of the clockwork army followed suit like a swarm of intelligent knives. I fought them off as best I could, but everything I grabbed sliced and stabbed me.

The attack lasted only a few moments and ended abruptly. I tried to get up, still desperate to save her, but could not move my limbs. I felt no pain, but a glance down at my body confirmed that I had been butchered, laid open in a hundred ways. As one the mechanical animals turned and stared at the woman.

I looked over, too, expecting to see her burnt and dying. Incredibly, it was worse. Flames engulfed the woman I had so recently embraced. Yet she did not burn.

No. She was quite at home in the crackling blue tongues that licked her naked shoulders and breasts. And—I can scarcely relate the depth of my disgust—the bottom half of her body had transformed into a thick, black and gold snake.

As rage distorted her beautiful face, a banshee scream burst my eardrums. Blue fire flowed from her eyes, melting the animals and trees, burning the walls, burning me.

I CAME TO IN THE woods beyond a barren field where the hospital had stood. Not a board or stone remained. Even the iron fence with its roses and thorns had melted into the earth.

I huddled in the dark, watching as police searched for non-existent clues. Looking down at my body, I found I'd been transformed into a ghoul: limbs burnt black, flesh falling from bone. Then, from the corner of my eye, I caught a movement—a white dog, eyes gleaming as it turned and leapt away.

Something burst inside me. A searing acid spread through every part of my body, the agony so consuming I couldn't even scream. The intensity caused me to hallucinate that I had become a massive python like her, engulfed in burning skin.

All night I writhed and twisted, rubbing myself against rocks, praying for death.

In the morning I woke to find myself naked and healed, skin as pink as a babe's. Of my physical injuries, nothing remained. My mental state took a bit longer to reclaim.

Over the next few days, I reflected upon all I'd seen and eventually arrived at the only explanation that made sense. I had discovered the truth that even the most pious priests never dared teach. The woman's true form, revealed by the flames, had given her away. The snake did not deceive Eve—Eve was the snake.

I knew the reports would say there were no survivors, because officially I had never been there. Her followers would concoct paranoid fantasies about her abduction, and contradictory myths of her ascendance. From such seeds religions are born. The truth would only make it worse.

The next day, my newspapers reported that Sleeping Beauty was a hoax. Other publications were enticed to follow suit. The doctors who had seen her were more difficult to convince, but as the saying goes, all men desire at least one thing more than they desire the truth.

I handpicked a staff of fifty to destroy or discredit any record of her: every copy of every article, every photo, every person who insisted on babbling about what they'd seen or thought they knew.

The expunging took many years, for she had a fierce hold on people's minds, but I relished the task. Strange how passion deepens when love turns to hate.

I even inserted fanciful stories about her in backdated editions of the European folk tales collected by Charles Perrault and the Brothers Grimm, along with fabricated reviews and scholarly analyses of these books in newspapers and journals. I must say, this stroke of genius tickles me even today. Indeed, my publishing company has proved to be the best investment I ever made.

And so, within a decade of the hospital's destruction, I'd completed the groundwork. Sleeping Beauty had been reduced to a fairy tale. Even my staff who had helped erase her memory had been erased. All that remained was to find her again.

True, I've been searching for a long time, but even this may be for the best. I've built a home for us deep underground. It began quite simply with the materials available back then: asbestos and brick. I'm not sure it could have withstood her power initially, but as technology has evolved, I've kept it up to date.

Now the walls are made of diamond nanorods. For myself, I've had a suit of aerogel made. Light and nearly invisible, I feel sure it can stand up to any pyrotechnics she can create. It almost seems unfair—the advantage science has over magic these days.

The greatest irony is that our embrace seems to have bestowed unnatural longevity, perhaps even immortality, on me. I have not aged. I need almost no water or food. My senses grow more acute.

You might mistake this vitality for a gift, but it's a curse. I can feel her, smell her, taste her—the lie of her beauty, sleeping somewhere in these woods.

Does she dream of me? Does she believe that like every other man who fastened eyes on her, my corruption is complete?

I hope so. I want to savor the surprise on her face when I take her home and wake her again.

This time I'll be ready.

# Medusa

AFTER YOU LEFT I TURNED to stone: marble woman at kitchen table. The cup of tea I'd been drinking when you looked at me for the last time cooled and began the slow process of evaporation.

This is it, I thought. Forever.

But even statues erode. Features, once chiseled, soften and blur. Ripples appeared and spread from my fingers to my arms—tiny movements that became perceptible only over time. Eventually, I learned to navigate my new body.

Next I decided to scrub the kitchen floor. After eons of staring at the same spot, I'd become intimate with every spill, crumb and hair.

The procedure, routine at first, assumed gravity as the vinyl remained stained. I tried bleach, Pine-Sol, even Comet. The scouring only highlighted thousands of small cracks and dents inflicted by shoes, appliances, claws.

Deciding there must be something better underneath, I pulled up the grimy vinyl to reveal green and orange linoleum, circa 1950. Very exotic. You would have hated it.

I slipped on a slinky ballroom gown and danced the cha-cha, imagining a dewy-eyed couple in patent leather pumps and wing tips gliding over this floor, once upon a time.

I'm of the belief that things and places hold traces of what was. Go to a Neolithic temple where people have worshipped for thousands of years, or the dungeon of a castle where they tortured prisoners. If you're not cold as rock, you'll feel it. And if those walls can hold the past, why not a floor?

For a while I enjoyed the linoleum, but then I noticed discolorations. Were they stains? The floor had been covered with vinyl for a reason, after all.

I grew obsessed. I imagined Patent Leather and Wing Tip entangled in sleazy affairs and screaming matches that led to bloody noses, spilled martinis and drunken sex on that very floor. No wonder I couldn't get it clean.

Not to assign blame, but this house was your idea. I liked the modern one we looked at, with skylights and open rooms. You insisted on history. And where are you living now? Some chrome and glass loft without any walls, high in the sky. Looking down.

VOWING TO ERADICATE ITS SORDID past, I tore up the linoleum with a crowbar and discovered pink tile, of all things. Was this house once the refuge of some sensitive Victorian spinster?

Maybe so. I spent the next week crocheting doilies and writing erotic poems thinly veiled by religious symbolism, content in my candlelit solitude, wearing high-necked dresses and corsets that kept my creeping passions contained.

That all ended last night when the wind rose to a howl. I found myself rippling through the house in a white linen nightgown, writhing against the windows and hissing at the sky. What with the billowing curtains and flickering candles, I nearly burned the place down. The pink tile had to go.

I shed my white gown, corset and frilly bloomers. Naked, I grabbed a sledgehammer and got to work.

It took me 'til dawn to smash the tiles and pry the slivers up, aching muscles and cut feet be damned. The longer I worked, the angrier I got at the former owners who'd just covered old floors with new. Didn't they know that hidden influences are dangerous?

By this morning I'd reached the sub-floor: pine boards, gouged and marred. Before pulling them up, I took a last look out the window.

All around me I saw houses, their bones obscured by paint, carpet and curtains like layers of veils. A knot of whispering neighbors dressed in sleek, gray suits and high-tech running togs darted glances at my house. I don't know what they saw last night, but there's no point in explaining. They wouldn't understand.

With the claw of my hammer I slid nails out of the subfloor, piling them in a tangle of twisted rust. Lifting the planks, I found under the joists a well of dark blue water, illuminated from somewhere deep below.

I stood at the edge of the water, dipped my ravaged feet and watched the blood wreath my reflection in spirals—red snakes dancing around the head of a woman I'd heard of only in stories. Lies.

The last bit of stone melted to flesh. Eyes wide, I uncoiled down into her blue light, shedding this house, this worn-out skin, this apocryphal life.

# What the Dalai Lama Said

JUSTINE CAREENED DOWN THE AISLE toward my cubicle, her scuffed, blue flats sliding over the industrial carpet like water bugs on a pond.

I'd only that moment sat down at my desk. I hadn't even taken my first sip of coffee. Call it a premonition, but I knew that whatever had Justine running faster than a goosed nun—I wasn't ready for it. I closed my eyes and took a deep breath as I heard her cross the threshold.

"Max! Max!" Justine said in a raspy stage whisper. "Are you meditating?"

"Yes," I lied.

"You shouldn't be talking, then!"

I sighed, opened my eyes and reached for my coffee, but froze mid-grab when I got a closer look at my friend. Normally she's cute in a kind of sexy librarian way, but today she looked insane. One tail of her rumpled, raw silk shirt had come untucked from her black skirt. Her spiraling hair, usually confined in a bun for work, rioted in all directions. Not only did it have a mind of its own, it looked ready to skip town.

"What's up, buttercup?" I took a noisy slurp of coffee.

Justine leaned across my desk and stared over the top of her wire-framed glasses. "The Dalai Lama," she intoned, "wrote back!"

I faked a vaudevillian double-take that got out of hand and I choked. Justine pounded my back with a mixture of concern and glee. After burning my tongue and dribbling coffee on my best white shirt, I managed to swallow.

"That's great!" I kept my voice low so as not to attract the attention of Delilah, office manager of Bullock and Stone Investment Strategies in Lynchburg, Virginia. Delilah couldn't have been more than thirty, but she reminded me of a Victorian spinster: thin, humorless and impatient, with a predilection for wearing muddy colors in the most hideous combinations. As my Daddy would put it, she could depress the devil.

When it came to Justine and me, Delilah's attitude of general dissatisfaction frequently escalated into a quivering pitch of barely-contained hysteria. Once, I'd overheard her saying that she thought it suspicious—a gay man and a gay woman spending so much time together.

"What the hell does that mean?" I'd sputtered to Justine later. "Does she think we're secretly straight and hiding it because, you know, the world is so intolerant of *hetero*sexuality?"

Justine had laughed and said Delilah probably hadn't been around many gay folks. "Maybe she thinks it means you hate the opposite sex. If she got to know us, she'd see we're regular people."

"Maybe we are, but *she's* not," I said. "More like a velociraptor having a bad hair day."

Now Justine flopped into the chair across from my desk and rummaged in her purse. "It's so awesome, Max! I mean, when I wrote the Dalai Lama I hoped, but I didn't really expect ... especially after all this time. But on the other hand, you know, the power of positive thinking ... so every night I prayed and visualized myself holding his letter, holding it right in my hands, and ...." Justine's voice trailed off as her purse rummaging intensified. Keys on a Rubik's cube chain, wallet, *The Idiot's Pocket Guide to Buddhism*, panty hose, prayer beads and a fair trade chocolate bar came spilling across my desk.

"No, no, no!" Justine moaned, and dumped the rest of her purse. Gum, tissues, a *Far Side* calendar and a glow-in-the-dark female condom with a bare-breasted Valkyrie on the package that looked like it had been riding around in there since spring break freshman year. "I can't believe it! I can't believe it's not here!"

"Where'd you see it last?" I said, smirking.

"I don't know, I don't know!" Justine tried to pace the cubicle, but could only take two steps in each direction. "I

didn't get it until almost midnight because the postman acci-
dentally—except there are no accidents, right—delivered it to the
downstairs neighbor. It was too late to call you, so I kept reading it over and over until about three a.m. Then I slept with it
under my pillow and this morning I put it ... I put it ...."

Justine rolled her eyes upward and held her hands out in
supplication. "Right! I put it in the pocket of my suit jacket,
but at breakfast Bad Kitty stepped in the butter dish, then
jumped in my lap, so I had to change clothes at the last minute and I left it! I've got to go home and get it, right now!"
Justine's voice had risen to a desperate wail and she started
shoving stuff back into her purse.

"You can't leave," I hissed. "You know Delilah's been
looking for an excuse to get rid of us!"

"But Max, what if something happens to the letter before I
get home? Bad Kitty shredded the newspaper again yesterday!"

Justine's eyes looked a little wild, so I grabbed her arm
and thought fast. Although I'd rather spend all day plucking
nose hairs than be at Bullock and Stone, the only thing worse
than being stuck in a windowless box, bathed in fluorescent
lighting and subjected to pointless tasks by narrow personali-
ties would be having to do it without Justine.

WE'D MET SENIOR YEAR AT Virginia Tech. Both of us were
business majors fulfilling humanities requirements at the last
minute by taking Intro to the Study of Buddhism, which we

figured would be an easy "A." Justine and I bonded over growing up gay in Lynchburg, though Justine had gone to the public school while I suffered indoctrination attempts at Liberty Christian Academy.

My folks meant well, but all the time I was growing up they thought the sun rose out of the Reverend Jerry Falwell's ass, circled the sky and popped back up his anus at night. To most of the world, Falwell was the kind of bigoted sideshow freak that gives the South a bad name. A caricature. But to a gay kid attending the church and school he'd founded, Falwell was the boogeyman come to life and foaming at the mouth.

My parents always got us to the cavernous Thomas Road Baptist Church thirty minutes early so we could sit near the front. I spent every Sunday between the ages of eleven and seventeen terrified that Falwell could spot the gayness in me like a wine stain on a white jacket and would call me out in front of God and everyone.

I managed to escape attending Liberty University by telling my parents I wanted to major in engineering so they'd let me go to Tech. Only problem was that in order to give substance to my ruse, I then felt obligated to actually study engineering for two long, miserable years before switching my major. When I prevaricate, I go all out.

As Intro to Buddhism had progressed, Justine's and my arrangement of sharing notes so that we'd only have to show up to class on alternate days developed into a mutual realization of just how deeply we were enslaved by the material world.

By the end of the semester, not only did we show up to every class, we had asked the professor for supplemental reading and joined a weekly meditation group. Our friendship blossomed around the shared hope that we could find a way to break through American cultural conditioning, which we now saw as the spiritual equivalent of giving children plastic bags and encouraging them to put them over their heads.

But underneath all that flowery hope ran dark roots of fear and twenty years of bad habits. I mean, when you've grown up on fast food, Internet, video games and recreational shopping, it's not like overnight you learn to be happy sitting on a hill wearing nothing but a sheet. And even say you did, your family and friends would freak out completely.

Graduation put an end to our days of tea and rumination, and we found ourselves back in Lynchburg. I was stuck living above my parents' garage until I could save up some money. It wasn't a Thomas Road Baptist kind of hell, but I wasn't exactly a free man, either.

Three months later Justine and I still hadn't come up with a solution to our philosophical dilemmas, and our new meditation group had disintegrated after the treasurer disappeared, leaving us more disheartened than ever. It wasn't the $347.25 she took; it was the principle. Et tu, Radiant Lotus (aka Tiffany Lipschitz)? That's when Justine decided to write the Dalai Lama for advice.

At first she'd been so excited, sure the answer was drifting toward us via international mail. But as the months passed with no reply, she'd gotten increasingly anxious and restless. She'd started talking about going to India, to Dharamsala where the Dalai Lama lives in exile. Justine said she could get the money for both of us to go if she cashed in some bonds her grandfather had left her. I thought about it, but when I found out that most of the toilets in India are holes in the ground I nixed the idea. My leg muscles just aren't that strong. But Justine wouldn't let up.

It all came to a head one warm April night as we sat on the roof of Justine's rundown apartment building, smoking clove cigarettes and staring at the James River reflecting moonlight in the distance. Justine announced that before going to visit the Dalai Lama we ought to purify ourselves in the Ganges River.

I frowned at her. "The Ganges is sacred to Hindus, not Buddhists."

"Since when are you so dogmatic?" She smiled. "Sacred is sacred."

"But the Ganges is full of sewage and industrial waste."

"Ganga is a living goddess. It's not her fault people have polluted her." Justine's chin jutted out in a way I knew meant she was fixing to get into it, but I was on a roll.

"If this world is an illusion, a big puppet show, it shouldn't matter where you are: India or Indiana. I don't see how slumming around a third-world country and getting dysentery is going to bring us any closer to enlightenment."

Justine shook her head. "I think you're just chicken to leave your safe little middle-class world."

"Chicken? What are we, five?" It was the same infantile accusation thrown by my ex-boyfriend Kevin when I declined to invite him home for Thanksgiving with my family last year. I wasn't hiding the fact that I was gay, exactly. My parents had eyes in their heads, but they wouldn't be comfortable talking

95

about it and neither would I. Besides, did I have to be labeled like a can of peas?

"Chicken," Justine said again. Easy for her to talk; her parents were Cooperative Baptists from Atlanta. They weren't happy when she came out, but after a tearful weekend they proclaimed they loved her no matter what. Two months later they were having dinner with Justine and her new girlfriend. Compared to the Moral Majority they might as well have been pot-smoking hippies.

"Why are you so fixated on the Dalai Lama, anyway?" I snapped. "Do you know what he said about sex? 'Right organ in the right object at the right time.'"

Justine looked pained, so I pressed my advantage. "Where do you think this doctrine leaves my preferred use of organs and objects? Or yours?" I'd meant to break the news to her gently, not use it as a weapon. But like I said, she'd pushed my buttons.

I'd been reading the Dalai Lama's books ever since Justine had become convinced he was the winch that could yank us out of our metaphysical quagmire. I'd really liked everything he had to say, too, up until that part about right organs and objects. It was depressing. If one of the most evolved souls on the planet didn't get it, what hope was there for mere mortals like my parents?

"Buddhist doctrine puts restrictions on straight people, too," Justine said, finally. "For example, they aren't supposed to have oral sex. But the Dalai Lama's compassionate. He knows people aren't perfect."

"Don't piss down my back and tell me it's raining. Being gay is not an imperfection!"

Justine blanched. "That's not what I meant!" She scrubbed her scalp with both hands, causing her hair to tuft out at tortured angles. "Since you know so much, you must know the Dalai Lama has spoken out against gay discrimination!"

"Yes, but he said that for a Buddhist, a relationship between two men is *wrong*. I might as well go back to being Southern Baptist and sign up for gay re-education camp."

Justine's eyes glimmered. "Maybe he's not perfect, but he's a great teacher. I just have this feeling ...." She shook her head and glared. "I can't go on like this. One way or another I'm getting out. You want to end up like Delilah? Bitter, flat, bored and boring? That's on you."

JUSTINE AND I DIDN'T SPEAK for three days. Even though we made up eventually, things hadn't been the same. I knew it was a long shot, but I was hoping now that Justine had received a response from the Dalai Lama she'd let go of her obsession with India. But first I had to keep her from going AWOL and bringing Delilah's wrath down on both of us.

"Please, you can't leave without telling me what the Dalai Lama said!" I moaned dramatically. "Besides, we've got 200 pages of the Berman report to transcribe, and Delilah has on her gray tweed coat with an olive skirt, brown tights and black shoes. You know what that does to me!" I was deadly serious about that last part, so by the time I finished my plea, genuine emotion had welled up at the thought of her bilious color scheme.

Justine squinted at me, gauging my desperation, then sighed. "Okay, I'll try." She paced the cubicle again, making me dizzy.

"Here, sit down." I guided her into the chair. "Breathe deeply ... again." Justine did as I asked, holding her hands in the Jnana Mudra.

"Now, what did he say?"

Justine smiled radiantly. "Oh, Max. He explained everything perfectly."

"Like what?"

"Well, for example, that people like Delilah are mosquitoes at a picnic. They don't buzz in our ears or drink blood out of malice, it's just who they are, you know? They have a totally different perspective, so they don't understand us, either. It's like trying to describe pizza to someone who lives on Mars and doesn't have a mouth."

"The Dalai Lama said that?" I frowned in confusion.

"Yes!" Justine glowed with happiness as she took another breath.

"That's odd," I murmured. "What else?"

"Oh, tons of things about how the world is an illusion, of course, so we shouldn't jump to conclusions. You know, like if you're riding in a car and you smell something bad, and you think it's your friend in the backseat? But if it turns out to be like a farm or a paper mill that stinks, you'll be really glad you didn't accuse her of farting."

"What?" I yelped, trying not to laugh.

"It's a metaphor," Justine said, smiling serenely. Closing her eyes, she inhaled and exhaled slowly. That's when I noticed her skin changing color.

At first I assumed it was a trick of the fluorescent lights, but they skew green. A moment later, it became obvious—her pale skin was taking on a luminous blue tinge, like a gas flame.

Justine opened her eyes. "Listen, Max! We have to pay attention to every single moment, even if it's totally boring or annoying or painful. We're always thinking that some other moment or day or year will be better, like kids waiting for Christmas, dying with anticipation, until finally Christmas Eve comes, only you're so wound up by then you cry over every little thing, like having to take a bath or pick up your toys, and you throw your plate across the kitchen because the mashed potatoes are touching your turkey, then you end up getting yelled at and you don't get to watch *The Grinch* again, and you go to bed feeling like your life is the biggest rip-off ever. And then for Christmas maybe you don't get the Barbie Fashionista you've been hoping and praying for, but instead you get something else like a chemistry set, which if you didn't get it you'd never find out your highest path is to be a scientist, and if you just stopped crying long enough to take a good look at the chemistry set and play with it a little bit you would realize this, but you're so fixated on wanting the Barbie that you're miserable, even though it's Christmas and you've got the perfect present sitting right in front of your eyes!"

Justine rose out of the chair slowly and turned in a circle with a strangely elegant gesture of her arm that seemed to encompass the whole office. "This is it, Max. Right here," she said.

I stared at her, unable to say a word. Have you ever seen a painting of a blue Buddha or one of those Hindu gods with all the arms? She was *that* blue. Swear to God.

I thought Justine saw it, too. As she reached out her hand to me, she started grinning like it was the most fantastically cool thing ever. I stood there and grinned right back, forgetting to worry about Delilah, forgetting how much I hated this place, or that I'd faked the letter from the Dalai Lama so that Justine could stop being so disappointed and quit threatening to drag me to India.

"Nirvana is here," she said, and touched my chest. "It's love, love, love."

I could feel her pulse through her palm, beating in time with her words. Or maybe it was my own heartbeat I felt.

I don't know how long it lasted. Just a few moments probably, but time seemed to stretch and inflate into a whole other shape. I remember feeling strangely euphoric, like flying in a dream.

Still smiling, Justine stepped back. Everything looked the same, but weirdly beautiful, too: the fluorescent lights, the coffee stain on my shirt, even the tacky furniture and office supplies, down to the paper clips and orange plastic ballpoint pens.

I'd always resented the fact that Bullock and Stone bought the cheapest pens on the market, then paid to have them labeled with the company logo—as if we might steal them despite the fact that they barely dispensed ink and ran dry after a few days of use.

I imagined the Lynchburg landfill heaped with all those plastic pens, their luminous orange bodies forming a tower of Babel that reached into the sky. This image, which normally would have filled me with disgust, now struck me with pathos, as if I'd known each pen individually, as if each one had a soul and aspired to something higher—tiny shoots yearning toward the sun.

Then the fire alarm went off, and Delilah's blown out and shellacked hairdo came floating along the tops of the cubicles. "Drill everyone! Let's go!" She popped her head in and glared at us. "Move it, people!"

She didn't seem to notice Justine's blue skin, or the beauty glowing like a sun inside of everything.

I WISH I COULD SAY that my life changed right then, that I knew what to do and what it all meant, but as the rest of the day passed, the luminous quality faded.

After work Justine showed me the letter, the same one I'd fabricated by cribbing quotes from the Dalai Lama's books—a wise, serene, sane letter, nothing like the zany rant that had burst out of Blue Justine. I'd written it with one of the Bullock and Stone pens, in fact, because they forced me to press so hard it made my handwriting unrecognizable.

"That was crazy today, wasn't it?" I said, tentatively. We sat at Justine's red and chrome kitchen table, drinking chai. Neither of us had mentioned the moment before the fire drill, and I had a strange, sick feeling, like when you're about to get fired or dumped.

"What was?" Justine asked.

"You know, just before the alarm went off? Your skin ... I mean you saw it, right?" My normally tenor voice rose into an embarrassing squeak, because Justine's forehead had that funny W-shaped wrinkle it gets when she's confused. "I mean, didn't you feel different?"

"Well, I felt really happy about getting the letter, but I guess it's not a magic wand. I still have to do the dishes and take out the trash, right?" Justine smiled.

*But you were totally freaking blue!* I don't know why I couldn't just say it. Maybe I didn't want to be the only one who saw. Not that Justine wouldn't want to believe, but deep down, would she? And what about the twenty other people she'd tell? It would turn into one more thing I'd be expected to explain and defend.

Also, I felt guilty about faking that letter.

Right after that, Justine got into Bikram Yoga and quit Bullock and Stone. She's happy doing her yoga and working at the health food co-op. She's happy meditating on the roof. She's happy cleaning up the messes Bad Kitty makes out of her newspapers and clothes. She's just happy.

I'm still working at Bullock and Stone, dodging Delilah and typing reports. When I move on it won't be to another job in Lynchburg. Call me chicken all you want. I'm going someplace where I can live simply, and where being a gay Buddhist is okay—so totally okay that I won't have to explain a thing. That's my idea of Nirvana.

But I'm not ready to leave yet. Being here connects me to that day, to that moment of grace. I've gotten in the habit of quoting the Dalai Lama out loud when I'm alone after hours. "No matter what sort of difficulties, how painful experience is, if we lose our hope, that's our real disaster." Or to paraphrase, Justine-style, "Even if your best friend achieves enlightenment right in the middle of corporate America and leaves you behind, you're only screwed if you stop believing it could happen to you, too."

I've decided miracles probably happen all the time, but people either don't notice or they have no way to process the experience, so they forget.

I keep moving the pieces around in my mind, trying to see how they fit: Justine's belief that the Dalai Lama could change her life; the letter, which was a lie, but also somehow true; and this office, a windowless hole that became holy for just one minute.

I keep thinking if I could remember that day better, I might be able to feel what I felt then. I close my eyes and see the lights gleaming off Delilah's hair as she snarled at us to move. I remember loving her in that moment (though never since), the way you love something that is completely alien yet perfect in itself, like a crocodile or an exploding star.

I remember Justine's skin, that vivid cerulean blue. I remember the coffee stain on my white shirt, shaped like a bird.

I remember the beauty of an orange pen.

103

# The Seduction of Forgotten Things

"Waving its row of lamps, the universe sings in worship day and night,
There are the hidden banner and the secret canopy:
There the sound of the unseen bells is heard."
—Kabir, *One Hundred Poems by Kabir*

ONCE THERE WAS A YOUNG woman named Isabelle who renounced her possessions. She kept only a change of clothes, black combat boots, toothbrush, towel, barber's scissors and a bottle of dark purple hair dye.

Isabelle hadn't always been a minimalist punk. Neither beautiful nor plain, brilliant nor dull, until the age of seventeen she accepted life as it came. But then one thing changed—just one—and this set off a chain reaction that untethered Isabelle from everything she'd been or had hoped to become.

It happened like this.

105

ISABELLE GREW UP IN THE capital of the Old South. Her family lived in a Gothic Revival named White Rose House, which looked old in order to blend in, but in fact had been built less than twenty years ago. The interior sparkled, modern and clean.

Until recently, Isabelle had long, dark hair and wore a different outfit every day, always in the latest style. She liked her pretty bedroom, done in blue-violet that matched her eyes. Her TV stayed on, filling her days and her dreams with fashion, celebrities, cars and news. But one day the screen just died.

Isabelle could still watch TV in the den with the lambskin rug, or in the stainless steel kitchen, or in her parents' white-on-white bedroom, or in the summerhouse out back. But when she went to bed she found herself immersed in darkness—something entirely new.

At first she left her iPod on so she could sleep. But then her dreams changed. She flew above the city at night, rushing water and wind rioting through her head. She tried turning off the music before she went to bed, but the dreams became more vivid. When she flew, the air sang across her skin. The web of city lights reflected a web of stars above, and she soared between them, following the curves of the river.

Isabelle felt as if her dreams had become real life, and she sleepwalked through her days. At Epiphany, the high school she attended, her friends teased her about the faraway look in her eyes. "Isabelle's in love," they speculated. "Tell us who it is!" But Isabelle didn't laugh, didn't reply. Soon the teasing turned to whispers. "Isabelle's acting weird."

It wasn't long before Isabelle's parents bought her a new TV. But now, when she lay in bed watching, expecting it to lull her to sleep, she found her eyes straying to the night-dark windows. Finally, she clicked off the TV and covered it with a sheet.

Not long after this, Isabelle's mother Mara returned from tennis one afternoon to find that her daughter's bedroom had been cleared out, emptied of the white wicker furniture, the thousands of dollars' worth of makeup, clothes and shoes ... and the new TV. Fearing they'd been robbed, Mara dropped her racquet and ran from room to room.

"Isabelle! Come here right now!" Mara shrieked. She'd discovered all of Isabelle's things piled in the third garage, where they stored their sporting gear. As Mara stared at the pile, something flashed by outside the window. One of the purple martins that nested in the rose garden, back from their migration to South America? No. Moving closer to the window, Mara saw her daughter running down the street.

When Jerome came home from work, Mara met him as he stepped from his car and dragged him into the storage garage to show him what their daughter had done.

"And that's not the worst of it. She's chopped off her hair and dyed it purple. Purple!" Mara squealed. She smoothed her own exquisitely highlighted, ash blonde bob with both hands.

Jerome nodded. A dapper bank president with silver hair and mustache, he'd seen a thing or two in his time. "She's trying to upset the apple cart."

"What do you mean?"

"The shabby clothes, the attitude. Reminds me of the hippies back in my day. Her school won't let her attend like that."

"Oh, they will. I told them not to get rid of the uniforms, but they wouldn't listen. Now we see where that leads." Mara plucked at a violet curtain crushed beneath a pile of magazines and DVDs.

Jerome frowned. "I suppose it's too late to send her elsewhere."

"She's graduating in three months! Only two classes left to finish."

"There's your problem." Jerome picked up a nine iron and hefted it experimentally. "Too much time on her hands."

"How did she even move all this in here?" Mara fumed.

"The gardener, I'll bet." Jerome shook his head. "He'll do anything she says."

"Fire him," Mara said. "I've been meaning to, anyway. I found fungus on my Aimée Viberts last week."

"THAT'S AN UNUSUAL DRESS, SUGAR," Mara called out the next day as Isabelle slid past the study dressed in a 1950s dress printed with illustrations of bees. "Did you get it at Vintage Style?"

"No," Isabelle replied. "The alley."

"Mmm," Mara said, distracted by some pink diamond earrings on eBay. "Is that a new boutique?" But Isabelle had gone upstairs.

A few minutes later, her mother knocked on the door of her room. "Isabelle, when you said the alley, you didn't mean ...."

"The dumpster behind the theater," Isabelle replied.

Mara nodded vaguely, eyes glazed. Her cell phone rang. By the time she'd finished discussing the details of her rose garden tour, she'd pushed Isabelle's incomprehensible confession clean out of her head.

---

Isabelle spent afternoons in her empty bedroom, staring out the tall, leaded-glass windows at the magnolia in the courtyard, the cobblestone avenue lined with stately homes from the Gilded Age, and bronze statues of failed generals on their mounts, charging the rebellious March sky.

Mara found her perched on a nest of blankets in the bay window, head cocked to one side. "What are you doing?" she asked.

"Thinking," Isabelle said.

"About what, sugar?" Mara tried to conceal the exasperation she felt whenever she saw Isabelle's purple hair and faded dress. "School? Boys?" But Isabelle only shrugged. Rebuffed, her mother stalked away.

Truthfully, Isabelle couldn't say. Her thoughts prowled in the shadows beyond the boundaries of language, their elusiveness darkening her mood. She waited impatiently to catch a glimpse of them, not sure whether she was hunter or prey. More and more, she didn't care. She only wanted to break through the veil that separated her waking life from the vivid and compelling world of her dreams.

Finally, Mara decided the best way to help her daughter through this crisis would be to get her interested in picking out new furnishings. "Of course, you needed a change." She nodded at her own insight. "You're a young woman now, and those were little girl things."

Although Isabelle greeted the magazines and swatches with apathy, her mother felt sure that a redecorated bedroom would set things right. So the next week Isabelle came home to find her room transformed into a blizzard of cream and white organza with a maple bedroom set and walls papered in chartreuse yellow fleurs-de-lis.

She refused to even step inside.

Mara pleaded with Isabelle to explain. Jerome accused her of ingratitude and possible drug use.

"Those things make me dizzy," Isabelle said. She took a pillow and blanket, and slept on the floor in the hall.

The next day, Jerome took Isabelle to see Dr. Bob Patterson, the family's physician and friend. An athletic man in his early sixties, Dr. Bob was always brimming with amusement at jokes only he could understand. Last summer he'd traveled to Nevada and set up an STD testing booth at the Burning Man festival. Recently he'd bought a $200,000 ticket for a joyride into space. Such behavior—social suicide for a less august person—left Dr. Bob unscathed. His was one of the first families, as they called those who'd arrived early to snatch land from the native people.

When Isabelle walked into Dr. Bob's office in an ivy-covered brick building on the grounds of his West End estate, he did a double take. "Oh my! Short and purple. What do your parents say?"

"They despise it."

"Yes, I imagine so." Dr. Bob grinned. If Isabelle hadn't known that he and her parents were the best of friends, she might have thought he took pleasure in this.

After Dr. Bob collected blood and urine samples, he and Isabelle collected Jerome from the waiting room decorated in walnut Queen Anne, and the three of them went to the club for lunch. By the time they returned, Dr. Bob's lab had delivered a sheaf of results.

"Well, you're in the pink of health, my dear!" he said, flipping the pages.

"What about her mind?" Jerome said, and Isabelle knew that this was the real reason she'd been brought to Dr. Bob— judge, jury and exemplar of the limits of eccentricity in her parents' group of friends.

Dr. Bob winked at Isabelle behind her father's back. "Well, I'm no psychiatrist, but she's a teenager. Damnable malady, but she'll grow out of it in time."

"Hmm." Jerome gazed pensively out the window. Whether this was due to fatherly concern or because a swath of the golf course could be seen from there, Isabelle couldn't be sure.

"What are you up to these days, anyway?" Dr. Bob asked. "Besides school and redecorating your head."

"Thinking," Isabelle said. Her father snorted.

Dr. Bob nodded. "I imagine you'll be off to college and into new kinds of trouble soon enough, eh?" He raised his eyebrows and his sea-green eyes bulged.

"I'm going to take a gap year," Isabelle said, smirking at Dr. Bob's antic expression. Unfortunately, her father turned around just then.

At home Jerome laid down the law. "You think this is a joke? Well, here's the punchline. In the fall you'll go to college or you'll get a full-time job. And that's final!"

"And you'll sleep in a bed," Mara added. "We're not animals."

"You may put a cot for me in the empty storage room off the kitchen," Isabelle said regally.

"Absolutely not!" Mara said.

"You can't force me to sleep in that bedroom with all those shiny dead things." Isabelle gave her parents a cool stare.

"As long as she keeps up her studies, I really don't give a damn where she sleeps," Jerome said to Mara. Disgusted, he left the room.

And so Isabelle was established in a cell bare enough for a monk, with a camping cot, a shelf for her meager things, and a door to the garden so that she could come and go as she pleased.

Isabelle began to walk the city every day after her morning classes concluded. Trailing her fingers down the old brick walls, she reflected that the people she knew treated the city like a wilderness. They scurried by car from country club to church, to school, to work, to the same old restaurants and boutiques.

On foot, Isabelle discovered that she didn't care for the busy streets. The noise and belching exhaust of the traffic jangled her nerves and made her long for sleep. The shop windows flaunting their shiny wares made her horribly dizzy, just as her new bedroom did.

She preferred the web of branching streets: the old, brick row houses with porches and balconies painted aqua, indigo, vermilion and peach. Better still, Isabelle loved the overgrown ivy- and moss-covered alleys where the city kept its unwanted things, some of them broken but many still usable. And these old, discarded things did not make her dizzy—as if the process of becoming dented, rusty and frayed had changed some essential quality in them.

Isabelle seldom touched anything but would make mental lists: rubber hose, rusted saw, mattress, beads, painting, keys, gas mask, cage, nails, plate, rope, basket, lamp. Once, digging down in the dirt to better examine a vase with the image of a snake-haired woman under the glaze, she unearthed a dozen screws that had been planted like seeds.

Wandering the alleys, Isabelle observed the men and women who spent their days combing through the trash. She admired them because they made use of unwanted things.

One homeless man in particular interested Isabelle. He had dark eyes, a scruffy beard and a long tangle of black hair. He always wore the same faded fatigues. Unlike the others, he didn't push a cart or carry a backpack. She never saw him collecting things.

He moved like the alley cats, appearing briefly and then vanishing into the leaves, until the morning she found him yowling outside Saint Francis Episcopal, a Gothic church built of river stone.

Saint Francis was famous for its bells, brought from England in the 1800s. On Sundays, six bell-ringers rang them in cacophonous, mathematical patterns called the changes. Isabelle's family had attended Saint Francis until the church got a woman priest and her father made them switch to Saint Paul's.

Isabelle had been contemplating some graffiti that read, "The truth will set you free, but first it will piss you off," in a nearby alley. When the changes started ringing, she realized that she'd missed the ordered chaos and exuberant volume of the bells—they seemed to scrub her mind clean. As Isabelle approached the church, she saw the homeless man yowling in throaty ecstasy like a panther in heat.

Ducking behind an old oak across the street, Isabelle watched the parishioners in their Sunday best emerge from church and make their way toward the parking lot around back. Some shook their heads. Others pretended not to see the man, though they passed within inches. The Walkers, a silver-haired couple in tweed whom Isabelle remembered, crossed the street to avoid him.

Isabelle popped out from behind the tree. "What's wrong with the man?" she asked, batting her eyes with faux innocence.

"Nobody knows," Mrs. Walker said. "They used to call the police. Just terrible, the sirens and lights, on a Sunday! But he always got away. Mother Anna said it was a sign that we must leave him alone to worship in his own way."

"The Walkers have always gone to Saint Francis," Mr. Walker declaimed. "I will not be driven from my house by women, soldiers or howling beasts!"

When the bells ceased, the man in fatigues stopped his serenade. He stood still, looking up enraptured, as if he was in love with the bell tower or the sky.

Nobody's ever looked at me that way, Isabelle thought. She crossed the street. Since the man had been oblivious to the churchgoers, she didn't expect him to notice her, but he did. For a moment the ecstatic joy on his face poured toward her.

"Hi," Isabelle said, smiling.

The joy in the man's face ebbed away, replaced by uncertainty. He spun around faster than she'd ever seen a person move and sprinted away. "Wait! I just ...." She didn't know how she wanted to finish the sentence, but it didn't matter. He had disappeared.

From then on, whenever Isabelle spotted him prowling the alleys she tried to follow, but he seemed to melt away. The only time she could be sure to find him was at Saint Francis on Sundays. Week after week, she listened to him howl with the bells. What was it Mrs. Walker had said? "Let him pray in his own way." That was how it seemed to Isabelle, too. The man was communing with something in a primal song of joy and praise.

Each Sunday after the bells stopped, Isabelle drew closer and tried to make friends. Each Sunday he looked at her as if he'd never seen her before and ran away.

Then one day, he didn't. He still looked afraid, but seemed to be waiting for something.

Isabelle realized that previously she'd started off trying to talk to him. This time she just waved. She remembered learning in school that this seemingly innocuous gesture had begun as a way to show strangers you held no weapon.

The man held up his hand, too.

Smiling, Isabelle pointed at the bell tower and clapped her hands.

The man's eyes lit up. The hint of a smile touched his lips.

*Ah. Now we're getting somewhere.* Isabelle crouched at the base of the dogwood that grew out of the uneven brick sidewalk and bent to examine the tulips growing there. A moment later, she felt him crouch next to her.

"Tulips always look plastic to me," Isabelle said.

The man frowned, confused, and Isabelle realized, *Of course! He doesn't speak English.*

"Flora?" She pointed at the flower.

"Flora?" the man repeated.

"Fleur?" Isabelle asked.

"Fleur?" the man repeated, still confused.

Isabelle sighed and shook her head. "I'm sorry; I don't know any other languages."

The man regarded her with heavy-lidded, slanted eyes that seemed more feline than human: feral but curious.

"Sky," Isabelle said emphatically, and pointed upward.

"Sky," the man said.

"Grass." Isabelle touched a feathery sprig.

"Grass," the man said, eyes widening. He was catching on.

Isabelle pointed at herself. "Isabelle."

"Isabelle," he repeated.

Now she pointed at him and waited, eyebrows raised questioningly.

The man hesitated, looking around at the things she'd named so far. It was then, pointing at his chest, that Isabelle noticed the frayed and faded name patch on his army jacket that read Alejandro.

"Alejandro?" Isabelle peered closely at his face. Under the tangle of long, black hair, he had bright hazel eyes. Under the sparse, scruffy beard, he had smooth, reddish-brown skin. *He's young,* she realized with a jolt.

"Alejandro?" the young man repeated, and smiled.

ISABELLE AND ALEJANDRO NEVER PLANNED to meet. Around ten o'clock, after Isabelle had finished her classes, she'd set off walking. Sooner or later he'd appear—except on Sundays when she would find him howling at the bells of Saint Francis.

Isabelle always watched from a distance, partly out of respect for whatever moved his devotion, partly because as long as the changes rang he stared into the sky, insensible to anything else. But when the bells stopped, he would turn and seek her with his eyes. And when he found her, he always smiled.

Most of the time they walked. They covered the web of overgrown alleys that ran behind the well-tended facades of upscale neighborhoods, bohemian enclaves and ghettos alike. It seemed that nature had been given a respite in these spaces between the named and tamed portions of the city.

Isabelle's habitual survey of abandoned things now became a teaching tool. Although Alejandro was learning English at a rapid rate, she still felt as if she'd tamed a wild animal. As they walked, she named and he repeated: couch, wire, book, plate, dresser, rug, jar, clock. They also practiced sentence construction.

"I'm tired," Isabelle said, pantomiming sleep.

"I'm tired, too," Alejandro replied. "In the sun I see you."

"Tomorrow," Isabelle corrected. "Tonight I'm going home. Tomorrow I'll see you."

"Tomorrow I'll see you," he repeated, frowning. Though language came easily, the concept of time seemed to confuse him.

For his part, Alejandro taught Isabelle the best places to shelter from the rain and how to find food. At first she refused to eat from the trash, waiting until she returned home at night to eat. But sometimes they wandered for eight hours or more, and when she began having dizzy spells, Alejandro became insistent.

"Good! Good food!" he'd say. Diving headfirst into a dumpster or trashcan he emerged with unopened cans, boxes of dried goods, cheese with only a bit of mold, loaves of bread, and produce with hardly a bruise. He began carrying a backpack with utensils and food harvested from the alley.

Until her change Isabelle had preferred fast food, and the combinations Alejandro offered seemed bizarre. Brie and orange-slice sandwiches? Spread made from canned salmon, goat cheese and pickles? Yet his creations tasted surprisingly good, and Isabelle's vitality returned.

IN JUNE ISABELLE TURNED EIGHTEEN. She graduated high school and was accepted to a private university in the West End. Her parents told themselves the worst had passed. They didn't know what she did all day, nor did they ask. Isabelle's credit card bill, formerly a tidy sum each month, had evaporated. "There's an upside to having an ascetic daughter," Jerome said dryly.

When the weather turned sultry, Isabelle realized she'd never truly experienced summer before; she'd simply shuttled from one refrigerated oasis to another. Her brisk explorations slowed to desultory strolls. On the first triple-digit day, her stroll became a miserable search for a shady spot with a breeze. The combat boots that had served her well until now felt like heated bricks on her feet. Then Alejandro appeared, dressed as usual in his long-sleeved fatigues. He wasn't even sweating.

"You're a freak of nature!" Isabelle exclaimed.

"What does this mean?" Alejandro asked, smiling.

"Aren't you hot? I'm dying of the heat!" She was acutely aware of the rivulets of sweat tricking down her neck and between her breasts.

Alejandro appraised her and shook his head. "No. If you are dying of heat, you are white and dizzy and fall down."

"It's just an expression," Isabelle snapped. "Maybe we should go to the library and work on your reading." They'd passed the massive stone edifice in their travels, and when the weather turned unpleasant she'd observed homeless people sheltering there.

"Library's closed," an old black man said. He'd appeared from behind an elderberry, pushing a shopping cart piled high with clothes and household goods.

"How can it be closed?" Isabelle asked. "It's Saturday."

"Closed on Saturdays." The man pushed back his fedora and wiped his forehead with a handkerchief, eyeing her as though she might be simpleminded.

Isabelle grimaced, trying to puzzle out the logic of a library that would close on the day when people would be most likely to use it.

Alejandro motioned for her to follow. "I know a good idea."

He led her down the alleys to a bridge that crossed a concrete canyon with a highway running down the middle.

Beyond this lay a neighborhood of tiny post-war cottages that Isabelle hadn't known existed.

At the end of the street, a narrow dirt path wound down a steep gorge to a footbridge. They crossed the bridge over train tracks and an old canal, pooling stagnant and green. On the other side, Alejandro and Isabelle continued down flights of concrete stairs. The lower they went, the cooler the air became. By the time they reached the shady floodplain, lush with ferns and old trees, her mood had soared.

Bisecting the city, the falls of the river ran half a mile wide, winding around wild, wooded islands. Although she'd lived her whole life only a mile from the river, Isabelle had never dipped a toe in it before. She'd only passed high above the gorge on bridges built for cars. Now she saw that the clear water ran across smooth bedrock and sand. Geese floated with their goslings, blue herons waded in the shallows, and osprey dived for fish.

Isabelle followed Alejandro down a snaking path along the river's edge. They passed groups of young people sitting on boulders or swimming. Farther upriver, they leaped from rock to rock over streams of bubbling water, arriving at a small, uninhabited island. There they followed a sandy path through woods overgrown with briars, ivy, wildflowers and grasses.

"Wow!" Isabelle exclaimed as the trees opened suddenly to an expanse of rapids and sky. The sun felt gentler here, its power diluted by the breath of the river.

At first Isabelle sat on the edge of a rock, dipping her feet and splashing her hands. Little by little, she waded farther out, holding her bee-print dress up around her hips. "It's not very deep," she reported.

Alejandro was squatting on a boulder above a small pool carved into solid rock, watching the water swirl around before it spilled into the river again. "Go down," he said, motioning downriver without breaking his gaze.

"What are you doing?" Isabelle asked.

He didn't reply, so she waded in the direction he'd pointed. The uneven rocks gave way to a sandy bottom and deeper water, nearly over her head. "Woo hoo!" Isabelle hollered and plunged in.

Isabelle let the current carry her; then she swam with all her might to get back to where she began. The dress hampered her progress, so she pulled it off and tossed it onto a warm rock at river's edge.

She amused herself by letting the river carry her down to one end of the hole, swimming back against the current, then surfing down again, until she heard Alejandro give a whoop of his own. She turned to see him holding a fat carp in his hands. "Good food!" he said. "Come see!"

Isabelle waded out of the river, shimmied back into her thin, cotton dress, nearly dry already, and leaped back to him across the giant rocks.

Alejandro showed her how to gut and skin the fish; then made a fire along a sandy stretch of river beach. While the fish cooked, Isabelle and Alejandro went to gather wild greens and edible flowers: chickweed, honeysuckle and lilac.

As they ate with their fingers, Isabelle decided that

Alejandro's delicate, colorful salad studded with chunks of grilled fish could have been served in her mother's favorite bistro—except for the cracked ceramic bowl and packets of dressing rescued from a dumpster.

She wondered, not for the first time, about Alejandro. What was up with the foraged gourmet food? Had he been some kind of survivalist chef? She'd often wanted to ask about his past but had held back, as if the wrong word could break the enchantment. *Who cares where he came from?* she scolded herself silently. *Pedigrees, resumes. I hate all that.* But the voice of curiosity taunted back, *What could it hurt to ask?*

"Alejandro?"

"Hmm?" He smiled at her over the salad.

"Where did you learn to cook?"

"What?"

She gestured at the salad and fish. "You make good food. Not everyone can."

He looked as puzzled as if she'd told him that not everyone knew how to breathe. "If hungry I look for food. So do cats, dogs, birds. But some food better with some other food, so I put them ...." He mimed his meaning by laying his palms flat against each other.

"Together," Isabelle said. "But you never had a job as a cook?"

"A job?" Alejandro frowned.

"Hmm." This concept had not come up before since Isabelle had zero interest in *that* subject. "It's something you do for other people, not necessarily because you feel like it, but because you want them to give you money."

"Money." Alejandro nodded thoughtfully. They'd found a dollar in the alley the week before, but she hadn't been able to properly explain why the dirty scrap of paper had value—not that she'd tried very hard. They'd been more interested in the wild carrots he'd spotted growing nearby.

"Okay. Say you have a salad and I want it," she began.

Alejandro stopped mid-chew and held the bowl out to her, but she shook her head.

"Wait. Just like, say, I wanted a pair of boots and you had some. Then I would give you money and you'd give me your boots."

"You want my boots?" Puzzled, he glanced at her perfectly good boots on the ground nearby.

Isabelle sighed. Abstract concepts were harder to teach than nouns and verbs. "Okay. You know how people live in houses?"

"Many people live in houses because of the rain." He snickered.

"One big house has more things inside it than you see in the alleys all week."

Alejandro widened his eyes and nodded his head. "A lot of things," he confirmed.

"Right. And the way most people get those things is they do a job for money. For example, I make food for you and you give me money. Or you have a house I want, so I give you money."

"I can trade money paper for a house?" Alejandro gazed up at a flock of crows floating by, black against the blue sky.

"If you have a lot," Isabelle said. "But everybody wants that paper, so it's hard to get."

Alejandro shrugged. "I don't need a house."

"Me either. I could live right here." Isabelle stood, stretched, and went to rinse her hands in the river. She stayed at the water's edge, squatting on the mossy bank, enjoying the feel of the water pulling at her hands. Alejandro came and squatted too, mimicking her behavior—a habit she found endearing.

Staring down into the clear water at the magnified pebbles and sand, Isabelle asked, "Alejandro, don't you remember anything about your past?"

He regarded her lazily with his cat eyes. "What, again, is past?"

"All the yesterdays. Back and back. What did you do?"

"I travel, but without you." He looked sad.

"But what about when you were a little boy? You must have lived in a house."

"I don't know." Alejandro sat back abruptly and took off his boots, snapping the laces. Isabelle wondered if she'd upset him.

As he stretched out his legs to dip his feet into the river, Isabelle spied a patchwork of pale scars across the bridges of his bare feet. Melted skin. She drew a sharp breath. Alejandro turned and caught the angle of her gaze.

"I can tell something," he said slowly.

"You don't have to," she said. "It doesn't matter."

Alejandro's eyes, lit by the sun, searched her face. She noticed they weren't solid hazel but gold with lines of dark green radiating out from the pupil.

He took her hand. "I want to tell you, Isabelle ... friend."

Isabelle found it hard to breathe. They'd never been this close before. She realized he didn't smell like most homeless people, piss and body odor seeped into clothes too long unwashed. He smelled like the river—loamy, green, and sweet with willow.

He seemed to be waiting for an answer, so she nodded.

Alejandro kept hold of her hand but turned his face to the sun. "Before you, I didn't know about yesterdays and tomorrows. Every day is today. Sometimes Here in this city, sometimes Here in the desert."

"You mean you traveled?"

"Yes. I am a traveler. Like that!" He snapped the fingers of his free hand.

"Hmm." Now it was Isabelle's turn to be puzzled.

"Many sounds and lights like police cars, but in the sky. Sirens! People ..." he opened his mouth to silently demonstrate a tortured cry.

"Screaming? Why?" Isabelle shivered.

"Fire in the sky, coming down. Burning."

Isabelle looked at his feet again, wondering how far up his body the scars went. She threw her arms around him.

Alejandro gasped in surprise, then put his arms around her and rocked gently, as if she were the one in need of comfort.

"Where is that place?" Isabelle asked. She loosened her grip on him, experimentally. He didn't let go, so she relaxed against his chest.

Alejandro shrugged. "Desert."

"What does it look like?"

"Brown people in orange robes. Flat sand, blue sky. Trees with leaves like this." He held his hands up in a fan shape, and then tucked them around her again. "Buildings painted white, round and low like women. Best part is the bells on top of all buildings. In the sun they ring. The people sing. Maybe I am a stranger because I don't understand the words. But I feel the bells and the singing inside. I fall into the sky and I'm Here."

It was the most she'd ever heard him say at one time. "So that's why you yowl like a cat at the bells?"

"What yowl?" he said. "I sing."

Isabelle stifled a laugh, but then another thought came to her and she pulled away to look in his face. "Was it a war? Were you a soldier?" She touched the name patch on his army jacket.

"It is a war, for all the todays. But I'm not a soldier."

Isabelle shook her head. "If you don't know where it is, how can you be sure it's happening today? You can't be in two places at once."

Alejandro frowned and pulled away. He rose and paced up and down the sandy beach. "You're right!" he announced finally. "You see."

Isabelle hugged her arms around her knees. "I don't see anything. I'm just asking!"

He strode back to squat beside her. "I don't know about yesterdays. I am Here in the green city; I am Here in the desert of singing bells. Understand?"

Isabelle nodded. "I think so. But—"

"I think maybe the desert is a yesterday." His eyes lit up with hope. "Since you are with me, I have not seen faces screaming because their skin burns, or because their children are dead."

*Had he been having flashbacks?* In her freshman year, Isabelle had seen a documentary about soldiers who'd served in Iraq. "Are you sure you weren't a soldier?"

"No, no. Never kill." He shook his head emphatically.

"So that's not your shirt?"

He shrugged. "Maybe I find it."

She felt vaguely disoriented for a moment but then shrugged it off. *The past doesn't matter. Only here and now.* She nodded. "What do I call you, then?"

He shrugged. "Any name. No name. Just traveler."

He smiled—gleamed, really, like a mischievous boy—and she thought of another question. "Hey, how old are you, any—" But before she could finish, he kissed her. And then the answer didn't matter at all.

When Alejandro let her go, Isabelle was so aroused she felt drunk. She touched his face, took a deep breath and kissed him again. His mouth tasted like the honeysuckle blossoms they'd been eating. Alejandro eased her down onto the sandy beach and stroked her skin. He seemed to intuitively know her most sensitive places—her neck, the inside of her elbows, the backs of her knees. She was shivering even before he lightly touched her nipples through her dress, teasing. Isabelle's bare feet floated in the river, and the silky water sliding across her skin added another layer of voluptuous sensation.

Just as Isabelle considered ripping off her clothes—and his—Alejandro broke away, stood and stripped.

She'd always thought he was skinny, but now she realized his clothes were simply too big. In fact, although lean, he had a healthy layer of muscle. The burn scars went halfway up to his knees, and the thick, pale, rippled skin contrasted with the smooth brown of the rest of his body.

Alejandro seemed perfectly comfortable naked. He made a show of laying his clothes on the ground in different configurations, trying to make a bed for them, with great flourishes and head scratching. The effect was both humorous and erotic, given his erection. Finally, he pointed innocently at her dress.

Isabelle pulled it off and handed it to him with a smile. He bowed to her and then laid the dress down in the gap. "Ah. That's what I needed," he said. He pulled her into his arms and this time he didn't let go.

Afterward they lay, heads touching, looking up at the sky as it deepened from cerulean to indigo. "This is the best day of my life," Isabelle said.

"My best day, too," Alejandro replied.

"How do you know?" she teased. "You might not remember your best day."

He rolled over on his side and gave her a worried look. "I know, Isabelle," he insisted. "I know!"

Isabelle's heart twisted. "I'm sorry. That was a stupid thing to say." She leaned over and kissed his cheek.

Alejandro sat up and frowned at the river. "I'll learn all the yesterdays, like other people."

"No!" Isabelle said. "Don't change. I like you the way you are."

"But no house ...."

"I don't want a house," Isabelle said. "I want to walk around the city and sleep by the river with you."

"For all the todays?" he asked.

"Yes!" Isabelle threw her arms around his neck.

They made love again, and then bathed each other in the moonlit river. When they got sleepy, Alejandro piled dried leaves and grass between two logs to make a nest. They lay together under his jacket, gazing through sycamore leaves at the flickering stars.

"That's my star," he said playfully, pointing at the brightest one.

"What's it called?" she asked.

He shrugged. "When I see it, I feel happy and safe, like a baby at his mother's breast."

"So you don't need these, then?" Isabelle asked, pointing at her chest.

"No." His smile glinted in the moonlight.

"Okay," she said. "I'll remember that."

"I don't need. I want," he corrected.

"Oh, so now you know English well enough to get cute?" Isabelle laughed.

"I have a good teacher," Alejandro said.

BY LATE OCTOBER, ISABELLE'S BODY had changed. Traveler, as she'd taken to calling Alejandro, teased that she was getting nice and round from all his good food. "You're like a cat in the sun," he said, because she didn't want to walk the city anymore.

"I have work here," Isabelle replied, gesturing at her new domain—one of the tiny, wooded islands in the middle of the river where nobody but geese and herons went. Even the near-est stretch of riverbank seldom saw the partiers, fishermen and families who sprawled on the rocks and sandy banks near the footbridge.

Isabelle hadn't seen many homeless people around, either. She wondered why. Perhaps they liked their privacy. Or per-haps, like their more affluent counterparts, they preferred the city with its abundance of things.

The remoteness of the island suited Isabelle and Alejandro. They'd set up housekeeping in the ruins of a stone building with two and a half walls and a tarp overhead that turned the light mossy green. They waded across waist-high water to get back and forth, and stayed put when heavy rain caused the water to rise. But Alejandro said that soon the river would be too cold, and in the spring, too fast and deep. They'd need to move or get a boat.

"Boat," Isabelle said, emphatically. "I want to stay here."

Alejandro made trips to the east side of the city, below the fall line where the river turned tidal and flat. He found several abandoned skiffs and tried to patch them, but each time he set one into the water it sank. He hung around the docks to ask the men where they found their boats. "Boy, you don't find boats. You buy them," the men said. And so Alejandro asked people to trade work for money. But so far he'd had no success.

Evenings, Isabelle and Alejandro built fires and cooked food, and Alejandro practiced reading out loud from books he'd found in the alleys. They started with *The Lorax* and *The Little Prince*. Within a week he'd graduated to *Native American Folktales* and a crumbling volume of poetry by an Indian named Kabir.

Isabelle loved to listen to Alejandro's voice, which grew more resonant as his reading skills increased. One night, belly full of olive bread scavenged from Sub Rosa's trash, Isabelle lay on the opposite side of the fire from Alejandro, enjoying the serenades of frogs and crickets.

As Alejandro leaned closer to the light, scrying the pages of Kabir's book, from her vantage he appeared to be inside the flames. *"There falls the rhythmic beat of life and death: Rapture wells forth, and all space is radiant with light; There the Unstruck Music is sounded; it is the music of the love of the three worlds. There millions of lamps of sun and of moon are burning; There the drum beats, and the lover swings in play."*

Alejandro stopped reading and looked up. Isabelle's breath caught at the sight of his eyes, liquid gold reflecting fire. "Do you like the poem?" he asked. "Does my reading please you?"

"Come here, Traveler," Isabelle murmured. "I'll show you." She rolled onto her back and stretched sinuously on the pillows she'd made.

Alejandro crawled around the fire and pounced on her. Wriggling together beneath the patchwork quilt, they licked and bit like two lion cubs until the heat began to rise and their play turned serious.

Sitting in Alejandro's lap with her legs wrapped around his back, Isabelle slid him inside her. He was exactly the right size. When their bodies merged, she always felt like a puzzle that had been missing a piece. That joining seemed to transform them into another creature altogether: a wild thing of tawny skin, claws and teeth, with tangy sweet and salty smells, and—shaken and tumbled at the moment of climax—a pair of enormous dark wings, unfolding.

They fell asleep still damp and entangled beneath the quilt. Throughout the night, Alejandro woke several times to feed the fire, and Isabelle resolved to finish another quilt, a warmer one, stuffed with the feathers from old down jackets. Suddenly, comfort had become, if not exactly a preoccupation, a compelling urge. She felt the changes in her body the way she sensed winter's approach, despite the balmy days.

Not that she was in denial. If someone had asked, "Are you pregnant?" she could have said yes. But since no one had asked, she hadn't translated the feeling into words.

---

Isabelle hadn't been home for months. The last time she went, she'd taken her warm clothes—black leggings and a faded orange sweatshirt with a hood—her towel, scissors and purple dye, and had left a short note. *Found a job, moving out. Love, Isabelle.* In her view, this was the absolute truth. Her job was to connect with the world.

On sunny days, she lay on her favorite flat rock gazing upriver into the hypnotic rush of water. In the distance, an arched stone bridge shimmered like a mirage. She never saw any cars or people venture across its span, so she assumed it had been abandoned.

The forgotten bridge charmed Isabelle. She vowed that one day she'd explore it, to see what made it sparkle like water in the sun. But for now she was supremely content to dangle her feet and hands in the river, not thinking, just listening to water and wind, and watching the shapes birds made against the sky, like the letters of an ephemeral language.

Then one night, Isabelle woke up sick and crawled off to vomit. Even after her stomach was empty, she couldn't stop heaving. Hours later she woke again, lying on the cold ground and shaking with fever. She tried to stand up, but her body felt like she'd been beaten.

"Traveler," she called. Her voice was barely more than a whisper, but he heard her and came.

She shivered and moaned as he carried her back to bed and wrapped her in the quilt. "What's wrong? Where it hurts?" he asked again and again.

In her mind's eye Isabelle could see the fetus floating inside her, but she couldn't speak. Then she became the fetus and everything disappeared. The last thing to go was Alejandro's voice, engulfed by a rhythmic, hushing wave like the pounding of blood in her ears.

ISABELLE WOKE IN HER BEDROOM in White Rose House. Sunlight splashed across the wallpaper of chartreuse fleurs-de-lis. Trying to orient herself, she looked around at the maple furniture, the cream organza drapes and bedspread, the cluttered dressing table. The TV across from the four-poster bed played a reality show about a family of women famous for their disasters in love and business affairs.

*I had such a strange dream*, Isabelle thought. *The most beautiful man. He loved me and I loved him. We lived in a crumbling castle by a river and slept on a mattress of dried grass and leaves. Now it's over and I'm trapped here again.*

Nauseated, she closed her eyes and rolled onto her side. Feeling something poke her arm, she looked and found an IV drip. She snatched back the covers and saw her belly, just beginning to swell.

Isabelle shot up in bed. "Traveler!" she screamed.

"Isabelle!" Her mother appeared in the doorway, wearing a white Lacoste tennis dress. "You shouldn't get up, sugar. Tell me what you need."

"Traveler." Isabelle kicked off the blankets and swung her legs over the side of the bed.

"Dr. Bob said you need to rest. Apparently you're in a delicate condition and you haven't been taking care of yourself."

"I take excellent care of myself," Isabelle snapped. She tried to rise, but a cramp hit and she slumped back onto the pillows with a whimper.

"It's time to stop being selfish," Mara said, grim. "That's what being a mother means. One day maybe your beloved child will leave you with only a seven-word note, and you'll know how that feels."

Dr. Bob walked in, looking like he'd just come from a round of golf, which he had. "Ah, good. You're awake." He gave her a crinkly smile.

"Get this needle out of my arm." Isabelle looked down at her lacy white nightgown. "Where are my clothes?"

"If you mean the tattered rags you were wearing when you arrived, they're in the trash," Mara said.

"Get them!" Isabelle gritted her teeth.

"It's too dangerous for you to go anywhere right now," Dr. Bob said. "You had a bad flu, but it was a blessing in disguise. The ultrasound showed a partial placental abruption. You've got to rest until it heals or you could lose the baby. Please, lie down on your side."

Another cramp seized Isabelle and she did as Dr. Bob asked. Before, the baby had felt like a part of her, like her hair or skin. It never occurred to her that it could cease to exist. "Please call Traveler," she whispered.

"And who might that be?" Mara asked.

"The baby's father," Isabelle said.

Mara shook her head. "Oh, Isabelle. I can't believe you've gone and got yourself pregnant by somebody with a name like that."

"Mama, please! Just stick your head out the door and call him."

"I'll do no such thing." Mara folded her arms.

"I'll go," Dr. Bob said. He left the room.

"Isabelle, I insist you tell me who you're bringing into our house!" Mara squinted her eyes—the closest she could come to a frown with her Botox-smooth face.

*A star man ... a panther I tamed ... a traveler from the desert of singing bells*, Isabelle wanted to say. But for once she was afraid to defy her mother—the stakes were too high. So she offered a plausible lie.

"His name is Alejandro. He's a veteran. Iraq or Afghanistan—I don't know which. He got burned on his feet and legs. He doesn't like to talk about it, so don't ask."

"But what makes you think he's lurking outside?" Mara went to the window and peered down at the courtyard.

"Didn't he bring me here?"

The look of horror on her mother's face almost cheered Isabelle up. "That filthy homeless man? He ... surely he's mentally ill. He was babbling about no water, no boats, no this, no that."

"It's Kabir," Isabelle said. "The poet. 'There is no water; no boat, no boatman.' I can't remember the whole thing. 'No earth, no sky, no time ... Be strong, and enter into your own body: for there your foothold is firm.' He must have been reciting ...."

Isabelle's voice caught at the thought of Traveler, who wasn't much bigger than she was, carrying her all that way. She imagined him struggling through the inky river, navigating unseen boulders while keeping her body above the rushing current. She saw him running down the twisting path to the stairs, climbing a hundred feet or more, and then trudging another mile through the city to her parents' house. And yet he somehow found the fortitude to remember and recite the poetry she loved.

Dr. Bob appeared in the doorway with a young man Isabelle didn't recognize. He had short-cropped hair, smooth cheeks, and wore a white Oxford shirt and khaki pants like one of the boys from school.

"That's not—" Isabelle began. Then she sat up and stared.

"I'm Alex," he said, tentatively holding his hand out to Mara. "Please to meet you?"

"Oh!" Mara limply held out her hand.

"Traveler?" Isabelle cried.

Composure broken, Alejandro hurled himself to his knees beside the bed and they threw their arms around each other, both talking at the same time. "Are you all right? Your hair! I didn't even recognize—I've been so worried—I'm so sorry!" They kissed hungrily, touching each other's faces as though reading information there. Neither noticed when Dr. Bob and Mara, embarrassed, withdrew.

When they returned a few minutes later, Jerome was with them. Alejandro tore his eyes away from Isabelle long enough to do his "Hi-I'm-Alex-please-to-meet-you" routine, which Isabelle found no less strange for having seen it already.

Jerome acknowledged him with a curt nod, but didn't shake his hand. Instead he said to his daughter, "I don't want to tell you what's on my mind, given your condition, but I hope you realize what you put your mother and me through with your disappearing act."

Isabelle stared at the wall. "I'm sorry if I worried you."

Jerome turned to Alejandro. "Are you responsible for this?"

"I'm the baby's father. I'll take care," he said nervously.

"What do you do?" Jerome asked.

Isabelle could see by the panic in Alejandro's eyes that her father had worded the question too vaguely for him. "He's looking for work," she said.

Jerome frowned. "Why am I not surprised?"

"I think I can help with that." Dr. Bob put a reassuring hand on Alejandro's shoulder.

"Thank you so much," Isabelle said with as much dignity as she could muster from her odalisque posture on the bed. "I never meant to hurt any of you. I was just out there living my life. To be honest, I want to be out there living it still. But if I can't leave yet, Traveler has to stay."

"Who's Traveler?" Jerome asked.

"Hi, I'm Alex. Please to meet you." Alejandro gave a toothy smile and stuck out his hand again. Jerome shook his head, but this time he accepted the handshake.

DESPITE THE AWKWARDNESS, ALEX, AS everyone except Isabelle now called him, slipped into the family with surprising ease. When he carried Isabelle down to the dining room to eat, she saw again his uncanny ability to mimic others, just a beat behind them. He took his cues from the way Dr. Bob walked, the way her mother poured cream in her coffee, and the cadence of her father's speech. Alex's effortless mimicry came across as natural to everyone except Isabelle, and it allowed him to blend in.

Mara gave Alex a guest room, but after the first night he slept in Isabelle's room and nobody objected. Dr. Bob secured a full-time job for Alex at Saint Francis, helping with the upkeep of the church. Best of all, the lead bell-ringer promised to teach Alex to ring the changes, so that he might stand in the belfry on Sundays in the charmed circle of six.

Alex brought Isabelle a plain, indigo cotton shift from donations at the church, and with relief she tore off her frilly white nightgown. He regaled her with stories of what he'd done and seen in the week that she had lain sick. "I climbed the magnolia so I could see in your window, and that's when I found a tiny house."

Isabelle smiled. "That was my tree house when I was a little girl." She stretched her legs, wiggled her toes and looked around the bedroom. She'd had Alex remove everything except the bed, but the floral wallpaper vexed her, so she rested her eyes on him instead.

He kissed her and pulled her close. "When I saw Dr. Bob come out with his bag of medicine, I jumped down from the tree. I told him I love you, and he told me about the baby." He leaned down to kiss her stomach. "Dr. Bob got me these clothes and took me to a man who cut my hair. Hair is very important to your people?"

Isabelle nodded. "Too damn important."

"Now we are the same," he said, running his fingers over her feathery pixie. "But no purple for me. Jerome said men don't dye their hair."

"That is not true," Isabelle snapped.

"Are you angry, Isabelle?" he asked. "Should I do purple?"

"No. I'm just pissed that I'm stuck here again." Isabelle glared out the window.

"You're a cat that wants to lie in the sun."

"I'm a cat that needs to fly," Isabelle retorted.

"Griffin!" He kneeled with one leg on either side of her tummy and held her arms out like wings.

Isabelle stared up at him. "That's true—part eagle, part lion. Where did you learn about that?"

"They have griffins on the bell tower." He got up from the bed and shut the door, shucked his polo shirt, unbuttoned his chinos and let them fall to the floor. Underneath he wore only his skin.

"Now there's the man I remember," Isabelle murmured. "But we're not supposed to have sex."

"Hmm." He took off her shift and lay down next to her, stroking her skin from head to toe, kissing her neck and breasts. She kissed him back and they touched each other until they came.

Closing her eyes, Isabelle pretended they were back in their house with the crumbling walls, and tried to hear the hush of the river in the sound of the central air.

---

On Sunday, Isabelle said she would scream if she didn't get outside, so Alex carried her downstairs and out to the summerhouse.

Though most dwellings in the neighborhood had postage stamp-size yards, White Rose House was built on several lots. This allowed space for Mara's prizewinning rose garden, with its circular brick paths and the screened house in the center. A twelve-foot wall shielded them from the eyes of the city.

After Alex left for his new part-time job waiting tables at The Tobacco Company, Dr. Bob came to check on Isabelle. He stayed for brunch and watched polo on the summerhouse TV. After crab omelets and several Bloody Marys, Mara took the opportunity to press for details about Alex.

"We want to meet his family, of course," Mara said. "Where do they live?"

"He's not in touch with his family," Isabelle said.

"Well, are they Spanish? Italian? Or what?" Mara shot her squint-frown at Emanuel, the new gardener, as if he might be to blame for Alex's dusky skin.

"He served his country and I love him. Isn't that enough?" Isabelle gave her mother a squinty look of her own.

"Of course it's enough," Dr. Bob said, lifting his mimosa in a toast. "We all support the troops, don't we?"

Jerome lifted his Bloody Mary in response, but his eyes were glued to the ponies on TV.

"Of course," Mara said between clenched teeth. "But that's not the same as welcoming the Unknown Soldier into our family."

"The Unknown Soldier!" Dr. Bob said. "Mara, you made a joke!"

Mara glared at him. "I don't see anything funny about it."

"My son loved that comic," Dr. Bob explained. "The Unknown Soldier, CIA, master of disguise. In later editions he became immortal, I believe."

"Bob, are you drunk?" Mara said. "I'm trying to have a serious conversation."

"I don't think I'm drunk." Dr. Bob swiveled his head experimentally and the polo on television caught his eye. "Well played!"

"Face the facts, my dear," Jerome said. "Isabelle's having a child with Alex. Would you rather she be a single parent?"

"Please stop talking about me like I'm not here!" Isabelle rattled the ice in the bottom of her orange juice glass.

Mara gave her a sharp look. "He's a janitor."

"They love him at Saint Francis. Intelligent, hard working, good manners." Dr. Bob took a sip of his mimosa. "I'm sure he'll move up in the world."

"Better than I expected from Isabelle, given her eccentricities," Jerome said to the TV. "No offense, my dear."

"Oh, no. None taken, Dad," Isabelle said with a sarcastic smile.

"Well, I see you've made up your minds, and I certainly can't fight all of you." Mara poured herself another Bloody Mary.

Isabelle ran her fingers through her short purple hair. "No one's asked me."

The three of them turned to stare at her as though she'd sprouted fangs and turned green. "Here we go," her father said.

Isabelle frowned. Trapped in her parents' house, she felt like a rebellious child again. She'd been terrified that they wouldn't accept Traveler—Alex—but now that they had, and so easily, she felt as if she'd been tricked somehow.

"Never mind," Isabelle said. "I should rest."

"Excellent idea," Dr. Bob said. "I'll carry you upstairs."

Isabelle slept until Alex came home at four o'clock. Then she ate a bowl of soup while he sat on the edge of the bed in his black slacks and white shirt, chattering about the lady from Saint Francis who'd gotten him the job at The Tobacco Company and all the tips he expected to make once he completed his training.

"Well, I made it all the way to the summerhouse today," she said, sarcastically.

"That's wonderful, my dear," Alex replied with Jerome's intonation.

Isabelle fixed him with a stare. "You're in with the parents, okay, Trav? You don't have to lay it on so thick."

"What's 'lay it on thick'?" he asked.

"Never mind. I'm getting better and then we can go home." Isabelle drained the last of her soup.

He smiled. "Yes, we'll get a nice house when the baby comes."

"The baby, the baby!" Isabelle mocked. "I want to go back to our island in the river. This week, or next at the latest. Promise me!"

He shook his head, helplessly. "It's not safe for you. You need to be close to Dr. Bob and eat good food, not trash."

Isabelle stared at him, feeling as if the air had been sucked from the room. "My God, we've ruined you." Although it had been years since she'd cried, tears burned her eyes.

"Shhh, no." Alex put his arms around her and kissed her cheek. "You'll see. I'll get you a house by the river. A real one!"

Isabelle would not be consoled. She lay curled around her belly as Alex dreamed out loud about the house he would get: oven, stove, refrigerator, dishwasher, furniture, dishes, drapes, crib, diapers, stroller, clothes, blankets, bottles, blocks, rattles, pacifier. But before he'd finished making his list, Isabelle had cried herself to sleep.

ISABELLE SLEPT HER DAYS AWAY, dreaming that she wandered the city again. Sometimes she flew above the shape-shifting river. Now it was a snake slithering through rocks, then a lover caressing her with his tongue as she floated in the dark.

Once Isabelle dreamed she visited Traveler's star. She saw round, white buildings glowing against the indigo sky. She saw women in orange robes. She heard the bells, their vibrations so intense she felt them in her bones.

When she awoke she found Alex, back from one of his jobs, watching her with the wistful look of a man staring through the lighted windows of someone else's happy home.

"I saw your desert," she whispered sleepily. "You were right. Everything rings like bells."

"Jerome thinks I must have been in Iraq." He bit his lip. "I wish I could remember more."

Isabelle propped the pillows under her back and turned on the bedside lamp. "In Muslim cultures the muezzin sings the call to prayer. No bells."

Alex frowned. "Are you sure?"

"They believe bells call demons, not God," she said.

He flopped backward on the end of the bed, eyes glazed. "So I'm not even a veteran. Just a crazy, homeless guy you decided to save."

Isabelle kicked at him under the covers. "You weren't crazy when I met you. I'm not so sure about now!"

He sat up, looking tired and chastened. "I'm doing the best I can for you and the baby, Isabelle."

"But I don't want any of this! Why do you think I chose you in the first place?"

Alex ran a hand through his short, rumpled hair. "I don't know. None of it makes sense. The way I used to howl at the bells, the way you appeared—ha!" He gave a harsh bark, so unlike his old, musical laugh. "I thought the bells gave birth to you. Now, tell me that isn't crazy!"

Isabelle stared at the wallpaper. The curling vines behind the flowers nauseated her but drew her eyes. "It was a logical assumption because I always approached you after the bells rang. You were a perfectly natural man!"

"I saw the way your parents looked at me the night I brought you home." Alex stood and paced back and forth in front of the leaded window. "I climbed that tree out there. When I saw my reflection in your bedroom window, super-imposed on top of your parents and Dr. Bob, I realized what I looked like compared to other people. I promised myself if you lived I'd learn to take care of you the way your family did."

She glared. "*Superimposed?* You have to stop this. I don't love you!"

He recoiled. "What?"

"I love Traveler," she said. "I want him back."

"Oh, Isabelle." He threw himself down on the bed beside her and immediately fell into a restless sleep, eyelids twitching violently.

Feeling as though she'd kicked a puppy, Isabelle turned out the light. She'd hoped to shock him out of the spell he'd

147

fallen under, but the next day he got up, showered, changed and went to his jobs. The day after that, he did the same.

Isabelle threw tantrums on a regular basis, screaming that she didn't love him, that he was an imposter who had broken her heart. Despite this, Alex insisted that all would be well after the baby came, as if her pregnancy was a form of dementia.

IN ISABELLE'S SEVENTH MONTH OF pregnancy, Dr. Bob pronounced her well enough to leave the house. "Don't overdo it or you'll find yourself on bed rest again," he warned, dashing off to his racquetball game.

Isabelle felt as dormant as the leaves and flowers. She'd slept her way through most of the winter, which her family had encouraged. Even Alex. To keep the peace, he kept to the guest room and went about his life, working two jobs, ringing the bells on Sundays, and taking business courses at night.

Isabelle surveyed her closet, stocked full of expensive maternity clothes. She knew without even putting them on that they would feel suffocating and heavy, whereas worn things seemed to breathe. Sighing, she put on her old socks and boots, and a pair of leggings under her indigo shift. Downstairs she borrowed the oldest coat she could find in the hall closet.

Outside, though the clouds hung like tattered rags, hope fluttered in Isabelle's chest. As she stepped beyond the garden gate, fat flakes of snow began to fall with a whispering sound. She walked slowly, one block down and back, through the whitening world. After spending so much time in bed she expected to be weak, but instead the motion brought blood back into her limbs and head. And the alley had a gift for her, spilling out of a cardboard box—a thick, blue and purple sweater coat, beautifully frayed.

Every day, rain, snow or shine, Isabelle walked a little farther. As she walked, the baby inside her leaped and kicked. At first this activity made her nervous, but then she realized that, like her, the baby had finally awakened. She had a traveling partner again. In her dreams Isabelle saw her daughter, a girl with caramel-colored skin and green eyes, splashing in the shallows of a sandy river beach.

Isabelle returned to the house a bit later each night, worried that someone would be awake, sipping port or herbal tea, a lecture spilling from his or her lips. But she always found the house asleep. Finally she understood. Caught up in their busy, whirling lives, Alex and her parents could only see what screamed for attention. Now that she had been pronounced well, they'd moved on to other things.

Still, the house squeezed Isabelle with the pressure of a deep, dead sea. She stayed because her one fear—that something would happen to the baby in the darkness of her belly—could only be assuaged by regular ultrasounds. But she longed for the time when she would hold the child safe in her arms and they could escape the suffocating White Rose House.

By March the dogwoods, redbuds and cherries bloomed, and the pale green leaves unfurled. The perfumed air, neither too hot nor too cold, felt like an extension of her body. Again Isabelle walked the maze of alleys, naming things—but this time to teach her daughter, still swimming in her private sea. Lunchbox, bucket, frame, book, dandelion, crow, bee. As she said each name, her daughter's voice echoed in her head. *Dandelion, crow, bee.*

Isabelle tried to guess her daughter's name. The baby said that she had one, but impishly refused to say what it was. "Mary? Lizzie? Luna? Denise?" Isabelle asked. No answer. It was none of these.

Isabelle also rediscovered the swollen river and marveled at the changes a season can bring. Where the earth had jutted out, it now curved in. Seemingly healthy trees had fallen. Willows and sycamores stood knee-deep in the muddy deluge.

Standing on the hill across from her island, Isabelle could just make out one of the stone walls of the crumbling house through the lace of new leaves. The longing to return surged inside her. "That's where we're going to live, you and I. Only another month or so, Cassie, Coral, Julia, Jan. The river will go down, and you'll be born, and we—" That's when she saw the silver rowboat floating in the marshy shallows, tied to a willow tree.

"Will you look at that," Isabelle breathed. She plunged into the muddy water and slogged over to the boat. It twisted and turned in the current, pulling on the rope as if it wanted to be free. Though a few inches of dirty water sloshed in the bottom, she couldn't detect a leak. Rainwater, she decided.

Isabelle untied the rope and dragged the boat out of the water. She slid it across the mud, concealed it under a thicket of vines and retied the rope securely to the base of another willow tree.

"There. All we need is a couple of oars. And I know where to get them." The third garage, of course, stocked with every type of sporting equipment. Then the realization hit her. "We don't even have to wait until after you're born. Once labor starts, that damn placenta won't matter anymore. You'll be coming out to eat and breathe. You'll be free and so will I. Free!"

*Free*, the baby said.

---

One day, wandering farther than usual in the hills above the river, Isabelle stumbled across train tracks almost lost in the weeds. She followed them through the woods to an abandoned bridge made of stone—the same one she'd admired from the island last fall.

Swinging her arms, Isabelle walked out into the green-smelling air above the river. The stones sparkled beneath her feet, and she remembered how she'd lain dreaming on her rock, wondering what gave the bridge its luminous quality.

Kneeling, Isabelle found that the bridge's stones contained iridescent shells and fossilized bones. "Look, Lark, Rita, Lara, Beth. Thousands of years ago, tiny creatures lived in those shells underwater, just like you. Now the animals are dead but their bones live on as part of these stones. That's how life goes, Helen, Carrie, Alexandra, Christine."

*Yes,* the baby said.

"Yes? Your name is Christine?" Isabelle raised her arms to the sky and spun in a pirouette. "I guessed!"

*Alexandra,* the baby said.

Isabelle dropped her arms and stood still. She'd become so accustomed to rattling off any name that came into her mind that she hadn't realized what she'd said. "Why? Of all the names in the world!"

*He needs me,* the baby said.

Isabelle's heart clenched with disappointment. "But I'm the one who's alone."

*No,* the baby said. *You have everything you need, but he's a traveler who's lost his way.*

"It's not fair," Isabelle said. "I gave you life. I lay forever in that horrible house so you wouldn't come too soon."

The baby didn't answer.

"I'm the mother, damn it!" Isabelle insisted. "You have to listen to me." But the only reply was the river's echoing roar.

All that week Isabelle stalked the alleys, arguing with her daughter. She explained how she'd tried to get through to Traveler, but to no avail. "I won't stay there, and I can't leave you alone with those people. You're just a baby! The stubbornest baby ever, true. But that won't get you far with them."

A homeless woman with fiery orange hair stared at Isabelle. "Keep it down, sis."

"You're one to talk," Isabelle muttered. She'd seen the woman before, engaged in loud conversations with invisible people. "I'm trying to discipline my unborn child," she explained, pointing at her belly.

The woman waved her away and continued digging through a bag of discarded clothes.

"I'm not calling you Alexandra," Isabelle told her daughter.

*You'll change your mind,* the baby said. *It's for the best.*

"You don't know what I'm going to do," Isabelle said. "Choose another name or I'll choose one for you."

This time the baby did not reply. And nothing Isabelle said from that moment on could elicit any response.

She tried to keep her spirits up, but she didn't understand how the girl could have sided with him. For that was how it seemed—another betrayal. And the silence in her belly chilled.

---

Isabelle returned to the bridge every day, listening to the wind whistling around the shells, whispering oceanic poems of violet and green. Nesting swallows dove at her, tails and wings streaming behind them like blue veils.

The bridge's crevices held echoes of the men who'd built it during the Depression. The woman who chose to end her life by flying off the bridge left something, too. She'd stood on the edge and made her last confession to the air.

Isabelle heard echoes of lovers in the stone balconies that hung between river and sky, whispering and kissing as the wheels of vanished trains kept time to the beat of desire. She remembered how in love she and Traveler had been, before White Rose House swallowed him, leaving only the glittering bones.

ONE MORNING A SIGN APPEARED in the woods, staked into the ground. "Railroad Property. No Trespassing." The grasses and vines that snaked across the tracks had been cut away. Isabelle's pulse rose. She walked onto the bridge, looking for workmen, but saw no one. A whistle tore the air, then a moment later screamed again. Closer.

Isabelle ran back into the woods, hid behind a tree and watched. Like an enormous steel worm the train inched across her bridge, grinding and squealing. Its mechanical noises drowned out the voices that had come to seem like friends.

She began to spend all her time on the hill, watching like a jealous lover as the train took possession again and again. She couldn't keep track of its arrivals so she finally asked Mara for a watch and a notebook.

It took a week for Isabelle to complete the timetable so that she would be able to visit her bridge without fear of meeting the train. Finally, one night when the moon was full enough to see by, she stepped out onto the bridge again, admiring its glittering stones and the rails that shone like two sterling bands.

Isabelle made sure to be nowhere around when the train was due. Other times, she sat on the edge of the bridge and dangled her legs over the unfenced precipice, listening to the bridge's voices. It was almost perfect—but not quite.

The train had tunneled its way into her head. At night, Isabelle dreamed of it charging her like a black bull. During the day, images flickered in her mind like a TV that couldn't be turned off—the train wanted something from her. She shuddered when she thought of its piercing whistle and pounding wheels, ready to crush anything in their path.

Isabelle remembered Dr. Bob once describing how as a boy he used to lay pennies on the tracks. On a whim she decided to see for herself.

The next evening, she set a coin on the track and waited on the hill for the train to pass. Afterward, the penny felt warm in her hand, flat and orange as the sinking sun and charged with the energy of the train. No longer a useless, anonymous thing, it had become unique.

Desiring something more complex to leave on the rails, Isabelle asked Mara for her silver baby cup. Flattened, it became a figure with arms outstretched.

Encouraged by Isabelle's sudden interest in heirlooms, her family urged their treasures on her. Mara made a gift of a pewter bell she'd been given as a wedding present, suggesting that Isabelle start a hope chest. "After all, you and Alex will be getting married soon," she said hopefully.

The train transformed the pewter bell into a silver crescent.

Jerome gave her a set of keys that had opened the family home his father had lost in the 1929 crash. Transformed, they became smoother and flatter, but they still looked like keys. Isabelle hung them from the edge of the bridge where they chimed together in the wind.

Alex told her that Jerome had pulled strings on his behalf and, despite the lack of any school transcripts, he was going to attend her father's alma mater. "Jerome said I'm like the son he never had," Alex said. "He gave me this!"

Isabelle held out her hand and Alex gave her Jerome's gold and ruby class ring. "Sigma Alpha Epsilon," Alex said like a benediction.

After the ring was sacrificed to the train, the ruby became powder ground into the gold, now shaped like a breast with a hole.

Tiring of metals, Isabelle left pillows on the tracks. She watched the feathers explode into the sky and float down to the river, singing.

Everything sang now: sycamore, pine, oak and ash, waving their leaves of translucent green; the grasses and wildflowers along the river bank; the sunlight by day, the moon and stars at night. Together they created a symphony: sometimes chaotic, sometimes harmonic. Isabelle felt she'd been deaf all her life and only now had learned to hear.

ONE MORNING IN EARLY APRIL, Isabelle rose at dawn. Stopping in the kitchen to stuff her pockets with nuts and dried fruit, she headed out the back door.

"Isabelle, wait!" Alex called.

Reluctantly, she turned. With the detached disappointment you might feel on observing the neglect of a house where you once lived, Isabelle noted that Alex was wearing designer pajamas.

"Can we talk?" he said.

"Later." She turned to go. The sun would be up any minute and she liked to hear its treble chimes as it rose, so different from the oboe sound it made at noon.

Alex put his hand on her arm. "Isabelle."

A flash of anger swept through her, and she pulled away with a violent jerk.

Alex looked embarrassed. "The baby's due any time. Please stay."

"No," Isabelle said. She ran out the back door, through the garden and out the back gate, her heart pounding. In the alley she glanced back over her shoulder. All clear. These days, Alex was probably too dainty to leave the house in his pajamas and track her through the alleys.

The next morning, Isabelle planned to leave even earlier, well before dawn. But as she passed through the dew-drenched garden, a shadowy form emerged from the summerhouse.

157

"You can't stop me," Isabelle said. "The baby's not in any danger. I know what to do when I go into labor."

Alex smiled. "Since you got well, you're feisty again. You'll be a good mother."

"Right," Isabelle said. "So I don't need you."

"But I'm going to stay with you, just in case."

Isabelle stalked out of the garden. She hoped he was bluffing. She hoped that in an hour or two he'd decide she was fine and rush off to class, or to one of his jobs. But Alex followed her all day, chattering incessantly about the baby (he wanted to name her Faye), their wedding (which she had never agreed to), and his plans to save money. Since he would be in school full time, he thought they should continue living at White Rose House. "I can finish school in three years and go work for Jerome at the bank. Then I'll be able to buy a nice house by the river, just like you wanted."

Isabelle didn't bother to argue, but she couldn't hear the sounds of the world anymore. Clouds moved in overhead like suffocating cotton, stilling even the raucous birds of spring. By mid-afternoon, Alex's talking and the oppressive weather had so frayed her nerves that she returned to the house and went to bed.

A contraction woke Isabelle at midnight. She slipped into her clothes and picked up the large backpack she'd prepared the week before. In the darkened hall outside her room, she tiptoed over Alex. He had decided to sleep there, bundled in blankets on the floor in case she needed him. As Isabelle passed, he muttered and rolled over.

The moon in the shape of a lopsided egg sang a high, sustained note. It shone so brightly she didn't need the flashlight she'd packed.

She'd walked her alley route halfway to the river when the next contraction hit.

*I'm coming*, the baby said.

"Hmph," Isabelle grunted. "Now you speak."

She sensed someone behind her and whirled around. The figure blended so well into the shadows that most people would think they'd imagined it, but Isabelle knew better. "Still have a few tricks up your sleeve, do you?" she muttered.

She ducked out of the alley and walked as fast as she could with her big backpack and belly, which felt heavier now that the baby had dropped. As she rounded the corner, her pulse leaped. There, in the hissing neon light of the convenience store, she found what she needed.

Isabelle approached the police car, pulling her sweater coat tight across her belly, and told the officer a strange man was following her. Then she continued on her way.

Looking back over her shoulder, she saw the squad car, its blue lights cawing like a crow with each flash, blocking Alex from following her across the road.

She figured she might have half an hour before Alex found someone to vouch for him and came after her again. By then it would be too late. She smiled as she thought of the silver rowboat tucked beneath the ivy, and the oars she'd hidden nearby. As if in anticipation of crossing the river, her water broke with a rush.

*Change*, the baby said.

Unconcerned, Isabelle leaned against a wrought-iron fence that rang like a gong. She shucked her leggings off, tossed them into a nearby trash can that trilled like a flute, and pulled a dry pair out of her bag. Despite Alex's interference, everything was going according to plan.

But when Isabelle arrived on the shadowy riverbank, the rowboat was gone. Only the fraying rope hung from the trunk of the willow tree. As another contraction hit, she sank to her knees. "Not yet, please!" she panted.

*Change,* the baby said again.

Isabelle got up, drawn by a new sound like a thousand vibrating crystal goblets. Wracked with pain, she couldn't identify the source, but it didn't matter. Her body had taken over and her body followed the sound until she arrived at the base of her bridge.

Isabelle had never seen it from below, but she felt safe under the arched stone legs that stretched above her into the sky. She pulled a sleeping bag out of her backpack and laid it on the riverbank. Next she laid towels on top of that. Then as another contraction hit, she collapsed. Kicking off her boots and leggings, pulling up her shift, she rolled over onto her side. Pushing, pushing, with a panther's yowling scream, Isabelle delivered her child.

Dazed, she sat up, clutched the baby to her and rubbed her with a towel. With a joyful squall her daughter began to cry. Feeling the need to push again, Isabelle lay back with her daughter in her arms and expelled the afterbirth.

Shoving the bloody towels off to one side, Isabelle pulled out her sterilized scissors and cut the umbilical cord. She dug a pale green baby blanket out of the pack, swaddled the child and climbed with her into the sleeping bag. Isabelle pulled up her shirt, guided the baby's mouth to a nipple and sighed with relief as her daughter began to nurse.

Lying back, Isabelle looked at the moon. Its sustained singing blended with the river's whisper, the bedrock's almost imperceptible hum and the ringing crystal tones. Despite the vibrant symphony around her, Isabelle felt numb. *Change*, the baby had said. Now she knew why. She could never leave her daughter, and Alex and her parents would never let them go. She was trapped.

*Not yet*, the baby said.

Isabelle rolled onto her side and propped the baby on her arm. "Why did you stop talking before?"

*You didn't want to hear what I had to say. And I needed my strength to grow. But now that I'm born, soon I'll forget how to make words in your head. This milk tastes so good and I'm so hungry! I'm already getting distracted.*

Looking down at the baby suckling in the moonlight, Isabelle wondered if she was making all this up. "Who are you?"

*A friend.*

Isabelle sighed. "You came for him?"

*Yes.*

"From the place where everything sings?"

*Yes.*

"But everything sings here, too."

*Because you remember, you're free.*

"I'm not leaving you." Isabelle pulled her closer.

*But if you stay, when I forget how to talk in your head, you'll convince yourself that I'm just a helpless baby and your mind will be lulled into forgetting again.*

"I don't understand," Isabelle said. Grief and frustration welled inside her chest. "Why do we have to forget?"

*That is how it is in this place. Almost everyone forgets. It's so sad. But the remembering part is beautiful, isn't it?*

Isabelle thought about White Rose House, full of silent, sleeping things. "That house is a mausoleum. I don't know how you hope to succeed."

*I'm very strong,* the baby said. *I think I'll remember.*

"And if you don't?"

The baby stopped her furious suckling for a moment, as if she was thinking, and then resumed. *If I fail, they'll send someone to help me. Maybe they'll send you. But you have to go now.*

Although the words vibrated with truth, Isabelle didn't understand how all of this could be. Her mind rebelled. "That's crazy. Whoever you are, you're in the body of a baby now. You'll die alone out here."

*Traveler's coming. He hasn't forgotten as much as it seems. But the others want to lock you away. They think it's best for you, and for me.*

Isabelle opened her eyes. Further down the riverbank, lights flickered along her path through the woods. The flashing beams sounded like rusty gates swinging in the wind. The sound told her to run.

Heaving herself up with a moan, Isabelle held the baby in one arm as she gathered the sleeping bag into a nest. She placed the swaddled baby in the center, turned the flashlight on and laid it on the ground beside her.

Isabelle took a long look at her daughter, with her feathering of dark hair and green eyes, and kissed her forehead. "I love you."

*I love you too, Isabelle,* the baby said. *Don't cry. We'll see each other again. Friends always do.*

The lights had moved closer, and Isabelle could make out the shapes of the people who held them. Someone yelled as they spotted her illuminated flashlight. Isabelle looked at the baby, who stared at her with solemn, focused eyes. "You're not supposed to be able to do that yet," she murmured.

*Run,* the baby said. Her voice clanged like the bells of Saint Francis ringing the changes. *Run! Run! Run!*

Isabelle ran. Barefoot and naked except for her indigo shift, she climbed the hill, concealing herself in the shadows beneath the bridge. The sounds around her had changed. The river chanted a reverberating bass, tree limbs buzzed like bees, and her feet sank into groaning mud. The sounds warned of danger, and this gave her the strength she needed. Shouts erupted behind her as the searchers found the baby.

At the top of the hill, Isabelle stumbled to the train tracks and followed them onto the bridge. Above the river she felt lighter, leaping from tie to tie. The bridge, glittering in the moonlight, whispered and sighed beneath her feet.

Safe at last, Isabelle crouched on the edge of the rail. She looked past her darkened island to the city beyond—the lights below and the stars above, part of the same bright web. Then the train track shivered beneath her legs.

Feeling as if she was swimming or dreaming, Isabelle moved toward the balcony at the edge of the bridge. She stood with arms held high as the train blasted through, powerful as a tornado, blocking the moon. Rumbles, squeals and vibrations made her belly contract in time to the pounding rhythm of the wheels. Rushing steel pushed air between her thighs. The air swirled inside her, hollowing her bones, until she rose and flew, borne skyward on the wake of the train.

Just before she disappeared, Isabelle glimpsed Traveler holding their baby, her skin reflecting the singing light of the moon. He reached up with his free hand in a motion that might have meant *Stop, wait!* or that may have been a wave, the ancient gesture that says, *I am your friend. Don't be afraid.*

# Purple House

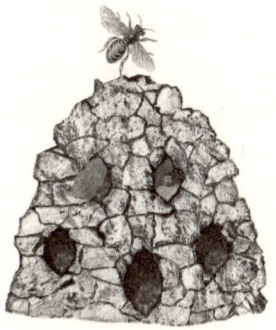

Excerpt from *The Metaphysical Tourist's Guide to Disputed Territories*, *4th edition, Marcus Shelton, Ed.,* "Chapter 12, The Balkans." 124–130.

## LOCATING THE HOUSE

The house squats like a cairn on the main street in Aggelos, an old city built of mountain stone layered on top of even older cities.

The village of Radomirë in Albania is the nearest town you can find on any map. Some travelers prefer to go from there on foot, absorbing the flora and fauna of the high altitude meadows dotted with sheep, and the sweeping vistas of shale and limestone cliffs. However, be aware that signposting is sporadic and you may encounter white wolves. Better to ask the proprietor of the pub to recommend a local guide willing to take you by four-wheel drive across the border into the disputed territory.

When you arrive in Aggelos, do not under any circumstances ask a local for directions to Purple House or you may find yourself escorted out of town. Simply locate the wide, cobblestone street that runs down the center. Follow it north, toward the highest peak in the distance, and keep a sharp eye out for the house with purple curtains. There is only one.

## WHAT TO EXPECT

As you step through the door, you are greeted by women wearing gossamer robes that reveal bare skin tattooed with tawny stripes. They kiss and hug you like a long lost friend, voices buzzing in a dialect understood only by them. They lead you through hexagonal chambers of red wax, strip you nude and sit you on velvet cushions in an empty room.

Other women who look the same, for they are sisters, serve mead and oval cakes that evoke the part of their bodies you most desire to see. Humming songs in a hypnotic drone, they dance in sensual, circular patterns, then withdraw behind the purple veils that separate the rooms.

Hours pass. You watch the sun penetrate translucent walls, for there's nothing else to do. Mead drunk, cakes eaten, you've been instructed through gestures and smiles to wait.

If you're the impatient sort, you may decide to collect your clothes from the heap in the corner and leave. Even if you're determined to stay, at some point you may find yourself chilled and cross, thinking, "This is not what I came for. This is not what I need."

There is an old Greek saying, *bees are born from the oxen.* It means no wisdom without sacrifice and pain. Just when you've given up hope of seeing the sisters again, when the house is so quiet you think they've gone and you're cursing yourself for a fool—that is when it begins.

You may have read other guidebooks that promise orgies of wine and flesh, archaic rites of ecstasy revealed. I have no wish to slander my colleagues, but if they've experienced the ritual themselves, instead of repeating rumors and myths, why do they fail to mention the most important detail—that it unfolds differently for each person who submits?

It might last an hour, a day, or weeks. But I warn you, if you want an orgy go to Thailand or Amsterdam. At Purple House you will be undone and remade.

## A BRIEF CULTURAL HISTORY

Albania, Macedonia and Kosovo all claim the mostly uninhabitable mountain range that holds the city of Aggelos in its lap like a jewel. However, after a series of bloody skirmishes that ended in stalemate, the three countries adopted the policy of behaving as if the region doesn't exist. This suits the citizens of Aggelos just fine. They have no wish to be dictated to by politicians who have never set foot in their town and likely never will.

In the old days, they called the house Mélissa Kypséli, Aphrodite's beehive. Now the old religion is the stuff of fables told by grandmothers, unfurled for tourists like a colorful flag. The name Purple House arose as a code, referring to the curtains—vivid, nameless banners that flutter against stone walls. The citizens of Aggelos no more acknowledge the Mélissas than they do the wind that moves through the leaves.

The women who live in the house have nothing to lose except each other, nothing to gain but the future. Their voices unravel like silken braids, undulate like hips, cascade like tears, rise and fall like breath. Their laughter, mingling with music and incense, pushes out the windows past the purple curtains and rises into the sky.

Housewives in the dusty street keep their heads down as

they pass, afraid to reveal their faces. The color of those curtains could stain their skin, the wafting aromas perfume their hair, make them dream of flight.

The air nearby vibrates, always, as if disturbed by wings.

## A Portrait, A Confession

Above the cobblestone street, sunlight skips across the rooftops and into the windows of Purple House. It careens through the upper rooms, slip-sliding across satin sheets, striped fur robes and smooth landscapes of skin, then skids around a corner and splashes against a red wall.

The youngest woman, passing through the hall, stops and leans her smooth cheek against the warm wax and smiles. She's in no hurry, even though a man waits for her in the next room.

Lying naked, he strokes the hair that runs down his chest and past his navel. He's tuned to such a pitch that he feels his body growing lighter. Time has stopped for him, but he knows the girl is near. He can feel the house now, every rustle and breath.

He is erect, of course, in the ecstasy of waiting.

The girl has met this stranger before. She knows his name better than she knows her own, which changes every day—Delia, Anna, Pandora, Jade, Venus, Mary, Hope, Grace.

The man is young and beautiful, old and fat, muscles taut, hands shaking, holding a weapon, caressing her hair. He kneels, begs, demands, weeps, laughs as he levitates into the air. He is a monster, a husband, a father—an average guy, like you, like me.

Nothing surprises the woman, young as she is. The house is an extension of her body. The house contains all she will ever need.

The girl sweeps back her hair, stretches against the red wall and bares her breasts to the warmth of the sun. Beyond the purple veil, alone in his room, the man still waits.

The girl waits, too, suspended in sunlight. Though she will die soon, she floats here now, content.

Unlike the girl, Purple House will never die. As the women become too heavy to fly, their daughters grow—vibrating, luminous—in an inner room. Even when the city crumbles, another layer in an archeologist's dream, the women will build the house anew—solid as stone, liquid as honey, airy as pollen blown by the wind that sweeps down from the peaks of Aggelos.

# Black Crater, White Snow

*JADE*

I SLIDE TO THE BARN on a skin of blue ice, sky layered rose and gray. Almost dawn.

The wind, a white knife, cuts through my red down coat. Pinfeathers escape—a flock of tiny geese vanishing into snow. The horses wear coats of icy beads; their breath makes veils of steam. As I pour the grain they blow and nip, bury their noses, grind yellow teeth.

We used to have lots of animals to feed. Sheep, cows, goats, geese. Now only horses. I lean my head on the black mare's back, breathe musky fur and dream. Leafy things ... drumming hooves ... hyacinth-scented wind.

171

I love the sound of my boots crunching snow. I love our house, oasis of green. I love the trees, hands that point to the sky. The trees and I watch for planes, even though Anna, my mother, says they fly too high to see. When a building or person explodes, they're already gone. But if nobody sees, how do they know for sure?

I don't ask. Anna worries too much already about the things she doesn't know.

You think your mother is so powerful; you think she can never fail. When you realize she's just a person, your heart cracks and a light comes out. It's love, the kind you have for fragile things.

In the yard the air goes still, flashes orange green. The horses shriek and kick the barn. Earth shakes, trees wave and I fall to my knees. Ice-crusted snow cracks in all directions—north south east west and down, down. A map leading deep.

I am not afraid to go.


## ANNA

WHEN THE RUMBLING STARTED, I'D just gotten out of the shower. Naked and warm, I wiped the fog from the mirror and stared into my mouth, trying to examine a tooth. As the house shook, my mind flashed back. I saw my teenaged daughter, Jade, buried in a gaping hole—a black crater a hundred yards wide in the snow.

I ran through the bedroom, my bare feet slapping the wood floor. The cold burned my skin as I pressed my face to the frost-etched window, but I didn't care. I needed to see Jade like I needed my next breath.

There. She knelt in the yard, a slender girl in a red coat, her copper-colored hair vivid as a flame against the snow. She was staring up, enraptured. I followed her gaze but saw only pale sky over flat, white fields—Iowa winter, barren as the moon.

I turned to survey the room. The pictures hung crooked on the green walls, but everything else appeared undisturbed. Under the mountain of white quilts on the iron bed, Lloyd Kopeck stirred. "Everything okay?" He ran a hand through his short, dark hair and stretched.

"I guess so," I said. "Could that have been a strike?"

"Just another tremor." He held out his hand to bring me back to bed and warmth.

I took another look out the window. "I should check on the horses."

"It's better if Jade does it," he said.

I flinched but it was true—I couldn't calm them anymore. Maybe it was the frequent tremors or the endless winter. Maybe they sensed my simmering rage. Everything was coming apart, hanging askew like the pictures on the wall.

"Come on." Lloyd motioned again, as if coaxing a nervous animal. I wanted to tell him he had the hands of a sculptor but he wouldn't take the compliment. He's a farmer, like most around here. Like me, too, though I hardly fit in.

Shivering, I slid under the covers, my cold flesh seeking warmth. Lloyd's fingers stroked my shoulder, moved lightly down my arm to my breast, circled once, skimmed my waist and slipped between my legs.

"No," I said. "I can't do this anymore."

"Yes, you can." His fingers fluttered inside me, arguing the point.

I groaned, tempted, but there was more—the hunger he couldn't fill with his body, the anger like a dark root.

I knew that after breakfast he'd go back to his people in Twin Tree. He'd shake his head, not saying much, but they've been expecting me to break up with him. My hair's too blond and my skin's too dark. I take lovers. Worst of all, I come from somewhere else—a cardinal sin in this small town.

Lloyd touched my arm as I pushed back the covers. "Why are you doing this, Anna?"

"Our travel permits will be here soon." I got out of bed and stuffed myself into clothes from the heap on the chair: long johns, two pairs of wool socks, and a flannel-lined satin robe.

"What makes you think things are better in New York?" Lloyd asked.

"They have what we need. Civilian hospitals, children's hospitals." *Psychiatric hospitals.* The thought came unbidden and I shoved it away.

Lloyd got out of bed and pulled on his long johns and jeans. "Have you been in touch with any of your friends back east?"

"I'm not good at keeping in touch," I said. "When I move on, I break clean."

"Like you're doing with me." He frowned as he pulled a thermal shirt over his head.

"This isn't about you." I picked up the silver hairbrush that had belonged to my granny and attacked my waist-length hair.

"Have you known anyone who actually got a travel permit in the past six months? On the net they say—"

"Commander Small said, 'The travel restrictions are for our protection, but there have to be humanitarian exceptions. Anything else would be insane.'" I glared at Lloyd and he looked away. "Spend too much time on the net and *you'll* end up insane," I snapped.

In the kitchen I put a pot of water on the stove for porridge. I make it from the organic corn I grow in my fields. When the water boiled, I grabbed the silky grains in one hand and sprinkled them in as I stirred. Breathing deep, I tried to calm down. There was no sense in getting angry with Lloyd. None of this was his fault.

The porch door slammed and I heard the stomp of Jade's boots. The frigid wind that followed her in chilled the back of my neck.

Jade came over and warmed herself by the stove, staring at the gas flame. She's as tall as me now, but not quite a woman yet. Her cold skin glowed blue against fiery hair. I cupped my hands around her cheeks to thaw them, and she looked up as if startled to see me. I tried not to worry that she was sick, on top of everything else. Even my olive skin was growing pale, needing the touch of sun.

First of June and still winter.

I ladled porridge into a bowl and handed it to her. She stood gazing into my face, green eyes singing as if I'd handed her a swan or an opal. But why?

"Are you in love?" The words popped out of my mouth, surprising me, but I hoped it was true. What a perfectly normal reason for a young girl to glow with such intensity, to stare raptly into the sky at nothing.

As she nodded I caught my breath. Was he kind? Would he love her back? A sly smile came to her lips and she pointed at her heart, then at me.

"Oh, you!" I hugged her; then shoved her toward the table. "Eat or you'll miss the bus."

Before the crater, Jade never looked at me like that. At thirteen she'd had little attention to waste on her mother, except to critique every decision I made.

After the doctors sent her home, I woke up every morning expecting to have my moody, talkative daughter back. But three months had passed and not a word. When she wasn't with the horses she wandered around, staring at ordinary things as if they held some magic key. When I asked her why, I got nothing but a smile and a wink like my granny used to do. "When the time is right, all will be revealed," she'd say.

As I watched Jade staring into her bowl with the fascination of a tourist, anxiety welled up again. The rare moments when she turned her laser gaze on me couldn't hide the truth—my daughter was drifting away.

## JADE

RAW SUGAR, SILVER SPOON. ONE, two, three into the grits.

"Go easy," Anna warns. "Or we'll go without, end of the week."

I widen my eyes to apologize. Forgot about rations again. In my bowl amber sugar crystals glow. Tiny suns casting light.

Lloyd walks in and stands by the stove. Anna doesn't turn. The set of her back says she's angry. Corn silk hair ripples in the folds of her blue satin robe. A frozen waterfall. She nods toward a bowl and a cup of coffee on the counter. "Eat before you go. It's twenty below."

Lloyd starts to speak, then stops. "Maybe you got it right, Jade. Maybe there's no point in saying nothing."

I smile, liking that, but Anna snaps, "Lloyd, knock it off."

"God, I'm just talking."

Anna bangs pots on the stove, "I know what you're doing. Leave her out of it."

I stare at their words, strung across the air like fishing line with glittering hooks. Puncturing.

Lloyd brings his breakfast to the table and sits across from me. I read his eyes and answer with a shrug. His time is up but he doesn't want to go. They never do.

Anna's spoon clatters in the sink. She turns and stares at me, her brown eyes two deep holes. She jerks her head and I follow it to my coat, vibrating red by the door. Orange scarf winds my throat. Light pulls me into silence.

No wind outside. Pastel snow reflects the hard blue dome of sky. Nothing moves. It's so still I wonder if the other world has broken through. I crunch across drifts that hide the lane, a quarter mile to the road. Looking for clues.

The road is a canyon carved deep. The bus appears, top level with the snow, tunneling like a worm. A humvee crawls behind, armored beetle with machine gun legs. They pull up and I wave. One of the legs waves back.

Still the same old world, I guess.

It's hot in the belly of the worm. Smells of wet wool, wet boots, barnyard rot. A senior named Otto climbs on, red cap sweeping the top of the bus. He's turned eighteen. Going off to fight soon.

"Hey, Rosie!" Joran Musser calls to Otto. Boys laugh.

In the seat ahead of me, Lucine Gorsky turns. "Do you know why they call him Rosie? Do you?" Her eyes, tiny chunks of coal. Unlit.

"They call him Rosie because he got a hard on in the locker room," Lucine hisses. "I'll bet your mother taught you all about that. I heard that *your mother* ..." Her face melts in the heat of my stare. Blood fountain. Bone sculpture.

I look out the window at sun on snow. Gold, violet, blue. It's only white when the clouds are low. You can see it if you look, but most people don't.

I learned how to see the day I got blown up in the crater. I was at the park in town, waiting for Anna to finish trading at the market. Dusk coming down. No wind. Cold air burned where it touched my skin, but I wanted to sneak a smoke.

I huddled on a swing and drifted in circles, thinking of Kegan, the boy with dark eyes who stares at me in homeroom.

His girlfriend Vera said, "When I give him a blowjob, he holds my head and watches." She said it casual, like "When I give him a cigarette ...."

I'd never done more than kiss.

She hates him watching, but I would hate him grabbing my head. Rabbit in a trap. Kegan hates me, Vera said. But if he hates me, why does he stare? I was sitting on the swing, wondering. Then a flash of light, the world exploded, and I flew.

From the air I saw the earth breaking free of snow, a dark mouth that ate swing set, merry-go-round, fence. Dirt rained and I fell with it, down into the hole.

In the crater I saw black horses running. A bearded man with ebony skin and brown eyes caught me, but he was falling, too. Faster and faster, arms and legs tangling. I couldn't feel the difference between him and me. Pleasure licked the backs of my knees, rose between my legs: a hundred-headed flower blooming in liquid waves. Was it sex? Death? Don't know. But I woke up in the field hospital, changed.

Some say a laser strike shot from a plane flying too high to see made the crater. Others say earthquake. The military says classified. Everyone agrees it shook the whole town. Anna ran to the park, screaming and searching for me.

They say if my coat wasn't red I would have smothered—left buried in the crater. The rescuers just saw the tip of my sleeve.

## ANNA

I HEAVED MY CRATE OF corn wine onto the counter at the market. Ralph Kahout pulled a well-chewed pen from one of the flannel shirts he wore layered like skins. He smiled like a man who thought he was charming; in truth, he smelled vaguely of piss. I wondered if the pipes had burst in the trailer behind the store where he and his wife Helen lived.

The market's five sparsely stocked aisles were empty of customers except for Wendy Yablonski and Rue Medved, rustling and clucking by the pot of dishwater-thin coffee. "Anna, did you feel the tremor out your way?" Wendy called.

I nodded curtly and turned my back, hoping they'd take the hint. No luck.

"You hear they're calling for more snow tonight?" Rue sipped her coffee, eyes bright with the prospect of spreading bad news.

"It's June!" Wendy moaned. "This keeps up we won't have no crop this year. Remember that Randol woman they used to have on War News Network? She said it's some kind of government weather-modification program. Haarp, she called it."

Rue clucked her tongue. "That don't make no sense. If it was a weapon, the Enemy Coalition would have bad weather, not us."

"Maybe it got out of hand," Kahout muttered.

"That don't explain the earthquakes," Rue said. "I tell you, it's the End Times."

Trying to tune them out, I glanced at the wall screen playing a net news feed. A barrage of images assaulted me: a carpet of dead bodies rotting on a tropical beach; a mangy dog, bag of bones, eating something that looked vaguely human; a mud-smeared soldier screaming, clutching the bleeding stump of his leg; brown-skinned children with distended bellies, staring bewildered at the snow.

The images came so fast there was no time to process them. No context, no sense. Revulsion clawed at my stomach. "Why do you show that?" I snapped at Kahout. "Half of it's fake."

"Yeah, but which half?" Kahout ran a hand over the stubble of his beard. "That's how they keep you hooked."

"Not me." I held my hand out for the credit and snapped my fingers.

He offered the slip, but as soon as my fingers touched it, he snatched it back, grinning.

I seethed at his childish power play, or attempt at flirtation, whichever it was. Served me right for offering an opinion. In a town this small, this trapped, any comment was liable to be taken as an invitation of one sort or another.

"So tell me." Kahout leaned closer, not smiling anymore. "Is half the truth better than none?" Something flickered in his eyes: a dispassionate, almost feral hunger I knew all too well. I'd seen it in the mirror.

"Not to me," I said.

"Well, it keeps most of the customers entertained, anyway." Kahout's grin slipped back into place. He handed me the credit slip, breathing over my shoulder while I checked the math.

As the wheels of my cart squeaked along the narrow aisle, Rue and Hilda continued to pollute the air with a stream of speculation. To tune them out, I mentally recited my list—*peas, beans, tomatoes, rice*—until Helen Kahout, furiously sweeping, stepped in front of me.

"Excuse me, Helen."

She straightened up, wrapped her hands around the splintered wood handle as if gripping a spear and bared her teeth. "How's the girl?"

"Fine, thank you." I looked her straight in the eyes and rolled my cart gently until it rested against her broom.

"Talking yet?" She shifted her weight and I noticed the dusty, gray flesh of her arm, settling.

"I'll be taking her back to New York to see a specialist soon."

"Hmm," Helen grunted skeptically. "I hope it's not brain damage. You know, that part of the brain that controls speech?"

"She still gets straight A's," I said. "Her English teacher says her writing has become vivid and mature. He wants to submit one of her essays to a competition."

I snatched a can off the shelf, threw it into the cart with a clang and pushed past Helen.

I'd lied. Jade's writing did show flashes of insight, but on the whole it had become fragmented and bizarre. When I asked where she'd gotten her ideas, Jade just stared at me with a mixture of hard-won patience and love, as though I was the child.

In the dry goods aisle, Helen materialized in front of me again. "Maybe she's just doing it for attention. Maybe she just needs a good whipping."

Reaching for a bag of rice, I pretended to lose my balance and rammed the cart against her shin. "Oh, excuse *me*!" I said, and barreled toward the check out lane.

"Say, got any more mulberry wine?" Kahout asked as he bagged my groceries.

"No mulberry, no apple, no corn," I lied again. "That was the last batch."

"Ooph. Good thing I've got my own stash." He winked. "Lot of people going to be upset, though. Even the Baptists drink these days."

I shrugged. Let them face this winter without my wine.

Since Jade got hurt, I'd begun to despise everyone: anarchists and terrorists, theirs and ours, who flooded the net with so much misinformation that the truth was hidden in plain sight; militias who fought our own military over the zone restrictions; ordinary people addicted to the never-ending stream of theories and conspiracies, like chickens pecking up feed. None of them were worth a damn to me. None of them could help Jade.

Outside, the deadly bitter air was a relief. I wanted to walk, but before I'd gone a block the skin of my face started to freeze. I'd left my scarf in the truck.

The post office wouldn't open for another half hour. I'd planned to go to the diner for a cup of tea but couldn't stomach any more rumors or advice. Instead, I walked back to my truck, turned it on and cranked the heater, wasting gas.

I should have seen this war coming. I should have planned ahead, but my focus wasn't what it used to be. Sometimes it seemed I could recall every sheaf of corn, every man who ever stood naked before me—making love, making crops grow. Then I'd look in the mirror and see myself as I am: a long way from my glory days, the hint of lines around my eyes, silver weaving into my hair.

It's an old story. The rise and fall.

I immigrated to this country because my people needed me. In Queens we lived as we had in Greece. Everyone knew their role in the rituals of planting, harvest and feast. But as my people adjusted to their new home, they changed. There was money to be made doing other things, and the city was hungry for land.

I stayed in Queens until the last of them moved on. They traded corn rows for row houses, farms for factories, fields for city streets. I couldn't blame them. The world was changing.

So I moved to Iowa with its millions of acres of corn. I felt sure that among so many farmers I would find new people to teach, but it didn't turn out like I expected. They didn't love corn; they loved yield.

Their god is science. But still, I didn't complain. Greeks are a patient people. When you've been around as long as we have, you take the long view.

I contented myself with what I had: a small farm with top-soil rich as chocolate, and my daughter, always hanging from my skirts or tangled around my feet.

Then everything changed again.

## JADE

AT SCHOOL, UNDER THE BIRCH where we go to sneak smokes, Joran sees a flock of sparrows, frozen. Boys throw rocks at branches until it rains dead birds.

"Birdsicle! Bird brick! Incoming!"

Above her thermal scarf, Margo's blue eyes narrow. "This is gross. I'm going in."

Cecelia gently tugs my sleeve. "Come on, Jade."

I shake my head. Margo rolls her eyes and turns away. Cecelia shrugs and follows. I watch them go, a little sad. We used to be a team. Pretty girls in pink and blue, cotton candy, strawberry smiles, freezing to something hard and true. But they don't understand.

Under the tree, bird spirits swoop and dive, confused. Flying dead. They turn into tiny blue lights. One flies into a little girl. Laughing, she runs in circles. The rest of the blue lights spiral—sparklers spinning on the Fourth of July.

I want to tell the others, "Look how beautiful! Look and see!" But I know better. The bird spirits dive straight down. Snow glows blue, melting to brown earth. Mini-crater. I look around. Boys throwing birds. Girls gone in. Nobody noticed the show except me.

Algebra. I finish my quiz, get a pass to leave class. I like to wander. I leap down the stairs so fast it's like flying. Death in her red dress flies with me.

I stand in an empty hall. They've waxed the floor, a slick, orange pool. The color makes a sound like a bell against the bright blue lockers.

Mrs. Heron, the vice principal, appears. "Jade! What are you doing out of class?"

As I hand her my restroom pass, I see a white ring of skin on the finger where her wedding band used to be.

"This pass says nine-fifteen. It's almost ten now. Are you all right?"

I nod, then notice four small bruises, yellow and green, on her wrist. Fingerprints. Crushed flowers.

She follows my eyes and stares at her arm. A brown cloud hangs on her skin. Sadness. I breathe deep, taking the cloud in.

She looks up. "Are you going to talk to us soon, Jade?"

I shrug and smile. Wait. She sends me back to class. Around the corner I run to the bathroom, blow Mrs. Heron's cloud out the window, watch it disintegrate.

Everyone is obsessed with talking. The doctor said I have post-traumatic stress, but I'm not scared or sad. There's just nothing I can say. They'll think I'm crazy if I tell what I know— I see another world behind this one, like a halo or a haze.

In that world, I'm a grown woman with skin the dark brown of newly-turned earth, wearing a long, red dress and a moon on a silver chain. I can almost hear her name in my mind, but then it slips away.

I call her Death, because after the crater I thought I'd died. When I asked, she said, *Alive, dead, it's really all the same.*

I guess that's why everything's gone so strange. I'm in love with silence, tree-shapes, snow, the curve of my mother's face.

### ANNA

AT TEN, THE POST OFFICE was still closed. I cursed Dave Mueller. He was open only three days a week; you'd think he could make it on time. Just as I was about to drive to his house and pound on his door, I saw his thin body hunch around the corner. As he gave me a wave, I pointed at my watch.

Inside, I gazed at the tarnished brass box, number thirteen. I could see an official looking envelope through the tiny window. This was it. I slipped my hands out of my thermal gloves and tore the envelope open.

It was from a doctor at the Department of Zone Security. I scanned. *PTSD ... antidepressants and therapy ... sacrifices ... freedom,* until I saw the words *request for transfer denied, for your own safety.* There was no phone number to call, no email address, no way to appeal.

A scream ripped out of me. I shook myself like a horse after a roll in the dirt, then kicked the front door of the post office with my steel-toed boots until the glass shattered.

I spun around. Mueller stood, horror frozen on his stone-white face. I knocked over shelves of envelopes, labels and boxes, and looked for something else to destroy, but the only table was bolted to the floor.

I raced to the truck, planning to go to the school and find Jade. Get on the highway and drive. I was scrabbling through my purse, counting the gas-ration coupons I'd been hoarding, when reason reared up. Eventually, the National Guardsmen would stop us at a checkpoint. They'd find out we'd left our zone, and then what? I saw myself naked under the olive canopy of a truck, a bribe on the icy road.

Could I do it? Maybe. But the next thought stopped me. It wasn't the prospect of bruises or jail or being escorted back, betrayed and leaking soldier semen. It was Jade's eyes that turned me home: green and changeable as the sea, recording every gesture and mood. Jade would know. Old enough to figure it out, too young to understand.

By the time I got to the farm, the sky had turned gray and the wind was rising. The National News Service confirmed the coming blizzard.

I no longer cared.

The horses were restless again. I could hear them whinnying and kicking the sides of the barn as soon as I got out of the truck. When I went to check on them, Guia reared and wheeled in circles. It was hard to look at her: shiny black coat gone matted gray, her face that used to nuzzle mine staring wild-eyed, as if at things I couldn't see.

I fed them corn and hay and curried their coats. Despite the lure of the grain, they twitched nervously under my touch, further darkening my mood. My horses, my daughter—all gone beyond my ability to understand them.

I spent the afternoon on the phone, trying to get through to someone in the Zone Security office. No one answered. I knew that even if I got through, they would just tell me the same thing they always did. "Once the travel permit application is mailed it's out of our hands." But I couldn't stop. I needed to talk to Commander Small, to throw his words back into his face: "There have to be humanitarian exceptions, anything else would be insane."

Finally, I gave up. I knew I should make bread, but the cold had gotten into my bones. I slid into bed under mounds of white comforters and let myself drift.

I dreamed I rode Guia across barren fields. As far as I could see, there was nothing except snow and stunted trees. I was running from men who'd held me hostage for what felt like an eternity.

I rode until my horse collapsed to the ground. When I dismounted, I saw that she'd died of old age. I looked at my own hands, wrinkled and twisted, and knew I was dying, too. When I woke, I felt as ancient as I'd been in the dream.

## *JADE*

LAST PERIOD. GYM. WATER VOLLEYBALL. They don't make me play, but I like the pool. An underground cave. Everybody in town chips in fuel rations to keep it heated for the swim team. The Twin Tree Tornados. I used to be on the junior squad, swimming butterfly, but I don't care about racing or games anymore. I just float at the end of the pool, watching the world underwater.

After showering I see Kegan in the dark hallway outside the locker rooms. He steps in front of me, blocking the way. I wait for him to speak, but he just glares.

I think he hates me, but Death rolls her hips and laughs. That boy's got it bad for you, she says.

"What are you smiling at?" Kegan mutters. He moves closer. I stop breathing. "Why don't you do things like other people?" His eyes search my face. "Did you knock your head in that crater, or are you playing a game? Got everybody fooled."

I want, oh, I want to touch his chest or the smooth skin of his arm, but I can't move. When I remember to breathe, I smell chlorine and shampoo. Underneath that something sharp and sweet ... new-mown hay and chocolate ... the tangy smell of boy sweat. I stare him in the eyes, swaying closer.

"Come on, Kegan!" Joran bellows from down the hall. "Quit messing with the freak."

Kegan flinches, face red. Starts to say something then stops, turns and sprints away.

I watch him go, then glare at Death. Got it bad for me, huh?

She nods like she knows.

*I don't need him*, I snap. *I have a man. He makes me feel better than that boy ever could.*

*Oh?* She winked. *Tell me, then.*

*I don't know his name. He caught me when I fell into the crater.*

She shrugs and her coppery-brown hair swirls around her shoulders. *He's my lover. But you're a virgin yet.*

My heart sinks. I could never compete with her. But then I remember: I *am* her. She smiles at my confusion. Knows what I'm thinking, as usual. Why don't I know all her thoughts, too?

*You are me and not me*, she says. *You're the unripe corn; I'm the seed, buried in the ground.*

I frown. *What if I don't want to be the unripe corn?*

*When the time is right, all will be revealed.* She flickers like a candle before it gutters out.

*What does that mean?* I ask, but she's already disappeared. I don't think I like her today. She's probably not even real. I'm probably crazy, like they say.

I walk to the bus, slow. Kegan sits in the back row. He whispers something in Vera's ear. She laughs.

I sit in the front seat as we go, watching snow drive down from the sky. The violet vortex drills the windshield, melts beneath the wipers' beat. I want to be sucked up by the storm, carried far away. Hidden until spring makes the world different, makes a different me.

Finally, my stop. The doors of the bus fold open. I stand slowly, back straight. Ignoring all the eyes, I descend into three shades of swirling blue dusk. Snow snakes across our lane, plowed this morning, drifting again. Needles of ice tattoo my skin. Crystals adorn my coat.

I am the queen of winter, floating home.

After I feed the horses, I watch Anna kneading bread dough, making black bean soup. I cradle the mug of tea she gives me. Inhale sweet jasmine steam.

My eyes follow the line of the floor. Worn, slanting pine boards, knots and holes. Lloyd promised to fix the foundation in the spring, but now I think the house will sink, put down roots, become a living thing. New rooms opening like petals on a flower.

Anna says our travel permits were denied, but swears we're going to leave. She wants a CAT scan and specialists for me.

I shake my head and write on my pad, *I'm fine. I told you. Don't worry, please.*

She reads and tries to smile. Nods but doesn't believe. I look into her eyes, lush with tears. Blue summer rain.

Death says when you love a woman who's afraid, pick up the brush and take the pins from her hair. Smooth gold currents wash away everything except soft bristles and the warmth of your body against her back.

After a while, Anna rises and I sit in the chair. Waves of pleasure ripple as the brush caresses my hair. She talks about her Greece: things tasted, things heard, things seen.

I close my eyes and her voice takes me there. Souvlaki and baklava. Elliniko, bitter-sweet. White sheep, blue sky. Horses. People plowing the fields, singing. Corn ripening, gold and green. The final sheath of the harvest, reaped in silence, laid at my mother's feet.

I open my eyes. Death flies in, kisses the walls, dives into the floor, reappears above the stove. She glows hazy orange. The sun behind the fog.

## ANNA

FOR THREE DAYS THE BLIZZARD raged. I just wanted to sleep. Trips to the barn were surreal. Two steps out and the house disappeared, erased by a void of swirling white. I clung to the line strung between the house and the barn, knowing that if I let go and took even a few steps away, I'd wander in circles and probably die.

When we lost electricity, I laughed. No phone, no net, no big deal. I'd given up hope of help from outside. We had plenty of food and wood, so our bodies would survive. For some this might have been enough. Not for me.

I can't even begin to explain what it was like, watching my child stare at a cup or a candle, a mirror, a spoon, in trances that lasted for hours. Every so often she'd scribble a note. Something like *black spider in the corner, it's love, do you see?* I couldn't stand to watch her but couldn't distract myself, either.

I found myself staring for hours into the fire, dreaming of spring. Instead of crops growing, I imagined barren fields that refused to yield, devastation on such a level that even those at the top would feel the pain. But even that soon tired me. Despair descended like the snow that covered the house, suffocating and thick, and I went back to sleep.

By dusk of the third day the storm had eased, so I let Jade go and feed the horses. I'm not sure I could have stopped her, anyway. The drifts were halfway up the kitchen window, covered with a hard crust of ice. I stood on a chair and peered out, watching her go. Before she got to the barn she stopped, crouched and stared; then she turned and trudged back to the house.

When she came in, she stood in the kitchen doorway gazing at the ceiling.

"What is it?" I asked.

Her eyes scanned the room for her pad. *Dead soldier pasture,* she scrawled.

I stared at her. Then I pulled on my parka and boots.

Halfway to the barn, I saw his green leg and black boot, disembodied against the snow. It looked as if he'd tried to make an igloo for warmth, but sleep had won the race. Jade watched as I grabbed his leg, pulled him out, and put a finger to his wrist. Nothing at first, then a flutter.

"Help me get him inside," I said.

We each took a leg and pulled. Behind us, the soldier's body slid and bounced over the snow like an empty sled.

## *JADE*

BATHROOM CAVE, CANDLELIT. SOLDIER LIES naked in our tub. Anna's gone to heat more water. "Yell if he starts to drown," she said.

Propane heater on high. Steam beads on green tile. Sweat drips down my back and between my legs. The soldier doesn't move. I hold my breath and check for a pulse. Still alive, I guess. I strip to my underwear to bear the heat.

At first the soldier looked old: eyes sunken, skin tight. As he thaws, his skin expands, hiding the skull again. He's not much older than Kegan, I think. I sit on the edge of the tub, dip my hand in the water, and touch between his legs. Feel him grow hard.

Behind the soldier's pale, sleeping face, my lover's face appears. Dark skin, dark beard, dark eyes. I laugh out loud, a strange sound. First time I've heard my voice outside my head since I went underground.

I slip out of my panties and bra. I feel Death rise into me. A slow undulation starts at my feet, liquid shimmy side to side. It rises from knees to hips, waist to breasts, neck to head. My arms stretch high. As I dance, the dark man winces. A good pain, I think. The skin on his chest puckers and rises. A scar in the shape of a key.

I step into the tub and stand above him. He's pointing straight up, ready for me. His chest barely moves with each shallow breath, but his eyes spark and glow. Orange and black, burning coal. I sink to my knees and press his hardness between my legs. The pain is sharp, but the key fits.

I sit still, staring at the wall of the tub. White grout around blue tile, a field of crosses in the sky. After a minute the pain goes away.

I look into my lover's eyes and move my hips in slow circles, start to feel good. Warm tide tingles up my legs, into my belly, across my skin. Vibrations cascade in waves. Liquid flower blooms again.

I stand, legs trembling. The soldier bleeds. Or is it me? I put my hand between my legs. In my palm I find six pomegranate seeds.

The door opens. Anna's face, horrified. She looks at the sleeping soldier. "Jade!" A booming roar overlaps her voice. The whole house shakes, the walls crack. The soldier screams awake.

Anna pushes me down, covers my body with hers. Together we ride the quake.

The room becomes still. Anna pulls me to my feet. Plaster icebergs float in the tub. The soldier's eyes are open, but I don't think he sees. His hands search for his gun. If he had it, he would shoot, I think.

His eyes blink and focus. He stares at us. At me. *Naked girls are not the enemy.* He looks down at his body and flails. He wants to get out.

I try to help him, but Anna grabs me. "You! Go get dressed."

## ANNA

MY MIND SPUN IN A sickening blur. *Jade, what have you done?* Day by day, she's further gone into some dark place.

I put the soldier in my bed and piled on all the blankets I could find, but violent tremors shook his body. "Who ... who ... where," he stammered. Panic lined his face like a map.

"It's all right," I said. "There was an earthquake, I think, but it's over now. You're safe."

Jade came in wearing in a red velvet dress I'd never seen before; her damp, copper hair curled down her back. She looked older, beautiful and strange. I took a deep breath. "Are you all right?"

She nodded and stood at the foot of the bed, staring impassively at the soldier.

"Have to get to base. Ten miles, northeast," he said through chattering teeth.

I tucked the ends of the blanket tighter beneath him. "You're confused. You're near Twin Tree, Iowa. There's no base here."

Then it hit me. I grabbed his sopping clothes off the floor. No rank or insignia, just faded fatigues like you could buy in any surplus store.

"You're militia, aren't you?" I said. "Fighting the zone restrictions."

His silence was all the answer I needed.

"Look, I'll get you healthy, give you money, whatever you want, if you'll help us get out of here. My daughter was hurt.

We need to get to New York to get her the care she needs. I promise to make it worth your while."

I heard Jade leave, slamming the door, but I concentrated on the soldier's face as he struggled to connect his thoughts to his mouth.

"Ruins."

"What?"

"Earthquake, tsunami," he whispered. His shivering stopped. "Last week."

I stood up straight. "You're hallucinating. It's the hypothermia."

"No." His eyes wandered around the room.

"Impossible! It would have been reported."

His eyes twitched toward me again. "On the net."

Then I remembered the rumor—one of hundreds I'd made a point to forget. "Lies," I said. "Are you an anarchist? What do you people want?"

"Truth," he said. His gaze locked with mine and my heart clenched. I saw it clearly. He knew ... something. But what? Then his eyes rolled back and he began to convulse.

"No!" I grabbed his shoulders and held him down. "Stop that!"

His body went limp in my hands. I shook him, blankets flapping like wings, and screamed in his face, "Not yet, God damn you! Wake up! Wake up!"

## *JADE*

I RUN INTO THE NIGHT, leaving the green house trembling with Anna's rage. Questions. Lies.

Clouds break to full moon. Ice glows blue. Except, in the field beyond the barn, there's something new. A black lake. I move closer to the darkness and find not water, but space.

A new crater, bigger than the one in town. Vast cavern with jagged sides, the bottom hidden deep in shadow. A warm breeze comes out of the hole, flings ice crystals into the sky. They mix with stars then fall, melting. I breathe deep and smell fresh earth.

I hear a cracking sound—world splintering. The horses have kicked the barn door down. Guia, the black mare, plows across the field, neck-deep in ice and snow. Breaking through, carving a path.

At the edge of the crater, Guia stops and tosses her head. Mane flying she leaps. The others follow, grow wings against the moon. They soar into the canyon and disappear.

I hear my mother cry out. She's calling the horses, calling me.

I remember when Anna worked the fields. Her sweat fell like rain, and where she walked life grew. Worry about me has made her old. But now I know what the black mare knows. We're the seeds of a new crop. We must plant ourselves before we grow.

My mother stands beside me, staring into the crater. I take her hand and feel her wrist, delicate but strong. The forelock of a colt.

## *ANNA*

AS JADE TAKES MY HAND, I realize we aren't wearing gloves. Strangely, I don't feel the cold. "Guia, Ginger, Ava!" I scream. Nothing. I can't see the bottom of the crater, only crumbling dirt and ancient granite. The horses must be dead like the soldier.

I look at Jade. She's smiling, and that scares me more than anything else. I don't know her anymore. Her face reflects the moon, luminous and remote.

I turn to look at our house, silvery-green in the light. I'd thought it was a prison, but if we'd left for New York would either of us still be alive? Suddenly dizzy, horror-sick, I fall to my knees.

Snow and death. Jade gone. What's left?

Jade kneels in front of me and touches my face. *I'm not gone, just changed.* I hear her voice so clearly in my head that for a moment I think she's spoken aloud. I grab her tightly and kiss her cheek. Something sharp and heavy bursts from my chest—sobbing or laughing, or both. I rock her in my arms so hard that we fall sideways into the snow.

When I finally let her go, I lie back and look at the moon. My fingers touch bare dirt. A warm wind rises from the crater, sweet with the smell of spring, and I realize the snow along the rim is melting.

I press my hands against soft earth. It feels like another child, returned home. But it was never gone, just hidden. Like

Jade. She's been speaking in her own way. But it wasn't what I wanted, and so I couldn't hear.

Jade sits up beside me. She takes my hand and pulls me to my feet. We stand on the edge and look down. Deep inside the crater, a hazy light glows, silhouetting horses running.

I wonder if I'm going crazy. That would explain how I can hear my daughter's voice in my head, how the horses survived the impossible leap. "Jade, am I dreaming or is this real?"

*Yes.* Her voice is clear, but what does she mean?

Before I can ask, she steps off the edge. I have to follow or let go of her hand. Instead I let go of everything else—what I thought I knew about my daughter, and about myself.

Step by step, we find our footing, following the horses down into the dark, new earth.

# Invisible Heist

IMAGINE A BANK TELLER. LET'S call her Esme. You know the type: slender, blonde, luminously clean ... except her fingers, which are coated with an invisible money-paste made of oil and microscopic flecks of dirt and skin. Still, she seems to shimmer pink and gold in the tasteful glow of recessed lights.

It's a slow Wednesday afternoon, and Esme's barely awake. The few customers flit in and out of her awareness like birds. Funneling money, she's a window through which power flows, more absence than object. A potential, now filled, now empty, as money passes in and out like wind, like water, like any symbol you choose.

Between customers, Esme shifts her feet, teeters on stilettos and almost trips. Just behind her on the floor, a large duffle bag has inexplicably appeared. She turns, bends, unzips it. Inside, a pink gas mask and a note: *Put this on, fill the sack with money, and don't press the alarm. We're watching.*

She looks around, sees a few innocuous-looking customers and fellow tellers, their murmured transactions soothing as ocean on sand. Esme waits, suspended, as half-formed thoughts appear and disappear like silver fish. Is this a joke? A test? A threat?

Then a strange smell penetrates her reverie. Her eyes lose focus. Vision darkening, she gropes for the gas mask, slips it on and gulps fresh air. All around, blurred motion as bodies fall. She eyes the red alarm button but doesn't touch it. They're watching.

Esme packs money into the bag. She empties her drawer, then the next, on down the line. What else is there to do? She's not sure how much they want and she's afraid to disappoint. When the sack is full she reads the note again, but there are no further instructions. Still, the thieves have not arrived.

Clutching the bulging sack, Esme floats toward the doors. Solid brass, impossibly heavy, yet they open. Pulling off her mask, she steps outside and walks to the intersection, squinting like a mole in the spring sun. What now? She can't connect these events into a recognizable pattern.

Finally, the simple longing for a cup of coffee propels her down the street. Tipping on her narrow heels, she passes granite office buildings, men in suits, the coffee shop, and a policeman. She doesn't stop.

Is she an accomplice? Not in any traditional sense. There were no meetings, no phone calls, no plan. Yet the sack of money, pressing against her like a lover's body, feels vaguely familiar. She imagines a beautiful, bearded man in an orange shirt, holding a twisted staff with wings. He's by the harbor gate. He's waiting for her!

Esme begins to run. Her feet slip and she kicks off the stilettos. She doesn't question how this has come to pass. She doesn't think of her husband, his tie reflecting the blue light of his computer. She doesn't think of their condo ticking quietly behind drawn curtains, or of the microscopic new life, a space traveler, tumbling through the darkness inside her.

There's no need for thought at all.

She feels the air force its way into her lungs, jagged and pure. She feels the sack of money bang against her chest like a third breast, bouncing in glorious, painful abundance.

The harbor, smelling brackish and sharp, opens before her. No man awaits, but it doesn't matter. The sunlight creates a path, reflecting off floating fast-food wrappers, syringes and cans.

Esme steps out. The soles of her bare feet skim above the swirling, dirty water. The sky transforms—blazing orange gold. Like an ancient god on a ship of light, the thing that awaits her rises up.

# Acknowledgements

Thank you to all of my writing professors, Marita Golden, William Tester, Laura Browder and especially novelist Tom De Haven who believed in my writing almost certainly before it deserved such faith. Thank you to poet Michael Fallon, and to the brilliant Drs. Vargish and Vargish who introduced me to Borges, Marquez and Cortazar, which I can say without hyperbole changed my life. There have been so many remarkable writers whose books have been an inspiration, far too many to name here, but Tom Robbins, Jeaneatte Winterson, Kurt Vonnegut, Elizabeth Hand, Neil Gaiman and Kelly Link leap to mind. Although I wasn't consciously thinking about Link's "The Faery Handbag" when I wrote "The Evolution of Reptilian Handbags," I have to assume that her story subconsciously planted that seed, because I've read her work with such deep admiration. Thank you to Sheri Reynolds, Dennis Danvers and Andy Duncan for your kindness and generosity, as well as for your books. Thanks to all the writers from the 6 at 6 Richmond writer's group, especially founding members Ann Archer, Lisa Jones Crowley, Leah Lamb and Nathan Long.

Thanks to webmaster Rowan Randol, and to Jill Ronsley for copyediting. Credit and thanks to Glenna Hansen for Frank Fish and The Fish Club and to Allyson Rainer for Bad Kitty. Thank you to all my beta readers for your invaluable feedback, especially Mike Henderson and Lee Boyes for also proofreading. Thanks to Dan Thompson for fact-checking the Korean War scenes in "Mr. Happy" (any errors that remain are solely mine), and to Lauren Colie, intern extraordinaire. Last and most of all, a giant thank you to Mary Boyes, one of the best editors a writer could have.